ALSO BY BRIAN DRAKE

THE DARK PASSAGE

SAM RAVEN
BOOK TWELVE

BRIAN DRAKE

**ROUGH
EDGES
PRESS**

THE DARK PASSAGE

PROLOGUE

THE WIND TORE ACROSS THE DOCKS, A BITTER LASH CARRYING the tang of salt and rust. And sudden death.

Sam Raven crouched low on the rooftop of a crumbling warehouse, his breath fogging in the frigid air. Below, the abandoned shipyard sprawled like a graveyard of industry—cranes loomed like skeletal sentinels, their chains creaking faintly as they swayed. The Black Sea lapped at the piers, its dark waves glinting under the flickering glow of a single dock light. Beyond the shipyard, a city's distant lights pulsed weakly, too far to offer comfort. The desolation pressed against Raven, a mirror to the isolation coiling in his chest. This mission, a favor for his friend Oscar Morey, was a tightrope and he was walking it blind. But the former gangster turned global intelligence broker needed a favor, and Raven couldn't say no to a friend.

He viewed the docks below through the lenses of high-powered binoculars. Every detail registered: the uneven concrete, pitted by years of neglect; the skeletal remains of a half-dismantled freighter; the uneven barking of a stray dog somewhere in the distance. The scene was too still. Too quiet. Raven's instincts, honed by a decade of operations in places like this, hummed with unease. Something was off.

A metallic clank echoed faintly from the far end of the shipyard—sharp, deliberate, and too distant to pinpoint. He froze, straining to hear it again, but the wind swallowed the sound.

"Spinou, you got anything?" Raven murmured into his com unit, his voice low. The Greek mercenary, stationed a quarter mile away, was Oscar's pick for backup, not his. Raven didn't trust him. Rumors of Spinou's reputation—whispers of double-dealing in Athens, a job in Istanbul that went sideways—danced in the back of his mind. Maybe they were true; maybe not. Oscar liked him. Raven told himself for the umpteenth time Oscar's endorsement was all he needed. But his gut said the opposite and there was no reconciling the two thoughts. Raven decided the only choice was to watch his back till the mission ended.

"Clear, Raven," Spinou replied, his voice smooth, almost lazy. "Nothing but shadows and rats. Antonov's still pacing like a caged dog."

Raven's jaw tightened. Spinou's calm grated.

Sergei Antonov, the Russian arms dealer they were here to extract, wasn't a mid-level smuggler. His FSB background made him a high-value defector, a man with secrets able to burn bridges from Moscow to Washington. He had secrets he wanted to tell. The secrets must have held value because Oscar wouldn't have bothered coming to his aid otherwise.

Through the binoculars, Raven watched Antonov below. The Russian stood near a stack of rotting pallets; he pulled his heavy coat tight against the wind. His pacing was erratic, a man caught between resolve and dread. A worn Soviet-era watch glinted on his wrist, its face scratched but ticking, a relic of a life spent in the shadows of power. Antonov paused, fishing a battered wallet from his pocket. He opened it, his thumb brushing over a small photo. Raven zoomed in, catching a glimpse of a young girl's face. Antonov's daughter, maybe. The gesture was fleeting but raw, a crack in the man's armor. Raven's chest tightened. Antonov wasn't just running from the FSB; he was running for her.

Raven lowered the binoculars, his mind churning. He and Oscar had forged a bond years ago. There was little Raven wouldn't do for Oscar, which was why he was on the rotting roof freezing his backside off near the Black Sea, bringing home a defector with a Greek mercenary he didn't trust. Loyalty was a rare currency in his world, and Oscar had earned it. But this job felt wrong.

"Spinou, tighten your sweep," Raven said, his tone flat but firm. "Something's not right."

"You're paranoid, my friend." Spinou chuckled. "Relax. We grab Antonov, we're gone."

Raven didn't respond. He tapped the comms twice, a signal to stay sharp, and shifted his weight, his boots silent on the gravel-strewn roof. His body was a coiled spring—lean, scarred, built for precision. His hands, steady despite the cold, checked the Nighthawk Custom Talon .45 autoloader holstered at his thigh. His eyes scanned the docks again, cataloging every shadow, every angle. The flickering dock light caught his attention, its rhythm off—three quick pulses, then darkness. A signal? A malfunction? He couldn't tell, but it gnawed at him.

Antonov resumed pacing, his breath visible in the chill. The man's resolve was fraying; Raven could see it in the way his shoulders hunched, the way his hand kept drifting to his wallet. If Antonov bolted, the whole op would collapse. Raven's mind raced, calculating risks. Extraction point was a mile west, a Zodiac waiting in a cove. Spinou's van was the primary exfil, but Raven had a backup route through the sewers if things went south. He always had a backup. Always.

Too many shadow wars had made extra preparation as routine as breathing.

The wind shifted, carrying another faint clank—closer this time, near the eastern cranes. Raven's pulse quickened, but he kept his breathing steady. His eyes darted to the source, but the shadows revealed nothing. He pressed the binoculars to his face, scanning the cranes' bases. A glint. Metal? Glass? His gut screamed ambush, but he had no proof. Not yet.

"Spinou, east side. Check it," Raven said.

"East is clear, Raven. You're hearing ghosts."

Raven's grip on the binoculars tightened. Spinou was either incompetent or lying, and neither was good. He replayed the Greek's words, searching for a tell. Oscar swore Spinou was solid, but Oscar wasn't here.

Below, Antonov stopped pacing, his head snapping toward the cranes. He'd heard it too. The clank. His hand slipped inside his coat, likely gripping a concealed weapon. Raven's pulse thrummed. Antonov was spooked, and spooked assets made mistakes. Raven needed to move, to get him to the exfil before the op unraveled.

"Spinou, get the van ready," Raven ordered. "We're pulling Antonov now."

"About damn time," Spinou said.

Raven's eyes narrowed. He tapped the comms once, a final check, and waited. Spinou's response came: a single tap back. It was protocol, but it felt hollow, like the click of a trap springing shut. The dock light flickered again, three pulses, then black. The dog's barking stopped abruptly. Raven's gut twisted. This was the calm before the storm.

He rose to a crouch, his .45 drawn, every sense razor-sharp. The mission was about to go sideways, and he'd be damned if he let it take him down.

SERGEI ANTONOV'S hands shook as he clutched his coat, the wind off the Black Sea slicing through him. The shipyard's desolation amplified his paranoia. Every creak of the cranes, every flicker of the dock light, felt like a predator's gaze. He glanced at his Soviet-era watch—2:17 a.m. Raven was late. Or worse, compromised. Antonov's mind spiraled to a memory from three days ago: a warehouse, where documented a Russian arms deal. Crates of AK-12s, bound for terrorists, gleamed under harsh lights. Information on the arms deal was only the start of the intel he had to deliver, and it was all on the flash drive in his pocket—a death sentence for Moscow's elite if it reached the West. He'd betrayed his FSB masters for his daughter, to give her a life free of their shadow. Now, standing alone, he wondered if he'd live to see her again.

A shadow moved near the pallets. Antonov's hand darted to the Makarov under his coat, but the figure stepped into the faint light—Sam Raven, his face hard, eyes scanning like a hawk's. "Easy," Raven said, his voice low, professional. "You have it?"

Antonov nodded, fumbling the flash drive from his pocket. His fingers trembled, betraying his nerves. "This—it's bigger than you think," he whispered.

Raven's eyes narrowed, but he kept his tone curt. "Hand it over. We move now."

Antonov extended the drive, his breath hitching. Before Raven could take it, a sharp crack split the air. Antonov's head snapped back, a red mist blooming as a sniper's bullet tore through his skull. He collapsed, blood pooling on the gravel, his eyes frozen in shock. The flash drive skittered across the ground.

Raven dropped to a crouch, pistol drawn, his heart

pounding but his hands steady. Shadows shifted in the darkness—five, maybe six figures, their red-lensed goggles glowing like embers. A kill team. Antonov had been burned before he showed up.

Silenced weapons flashed, bullets chewing through the pallets. Raven dove behind a rusted container, the metal groaning as rounds sparked off its surface. He tucked the flash drive into a hidden pocket inside his jacket, its weight a reminder of the mission's cost. Antonov's words echoed: *bigger than you think*. This wasn't just a hit; it was a cover-up.

The kill team advanced, their movements precise, professional. Raven's instincts took over. He leaned out, squeezing off two shots. The flashes from the .45 and a hard-hitting hollow-points zeroed on target. The first hit a gunman's throat; the second punched through a red-lensed goggle. Both dropped, but the others fanned out, their silenced rifles spitting death. The acrid smell of gunpowder filled the air, mingling with the sea's salt tang. Raven used the containers' shadows, slipping between them, his mind mapping the terrain. The dock light flickered again—three pulses, a signal he now knew was theirs.

A figure lunged from the dark, a knife glinting in his fist. Raven caught the wrist mid-strike, twisting until it snapped. The attacker was a wiry man with a Spetsnaz tattoo on his neck. He let out a wail of pain, but Raven silenced him, slamming his head against the container's edge. His skull cracked and his eyes rolled back. The body slumped, and Raven moved before the dead man hit the ground, his breath steady despite the chaos. He needed the flash drive secured. He needed to honor Antonov's sacrifice.

He kept moving. A bullet grazed his shoulder, burning like fire, but he rolled behind a crane's base, shooting back with three rapid blasts from the Nighthawk pistol. Another gunman fell, a clean headshot with two more in his chest. Three left, maybe four.

A new voice cut through the gunfire, calm, accented, chilling. "Raven! Give us the memory stick!" A tall figure stepped forward, his smirk visible even in the dark. His silenced pistol probed ahead.

Raven's blood ran cold. The man knew his name, but Raven had no such advantage. No time to dwell. The Russian fired, the round clipping Raven's thigh. Pain flared, but Raven fired back. The .45 thundered again. The slugs smacked into the Russian's chest, a wet crunch as bullets hit bone. The smirk faded; the man crumpled.

Bullets ripped through the container above him, pinning him down. The kill team tightened their net, their red goggles scanning like predators. Raven's odds were grim—three against one, wounded, exposed. He slapped a new mag into the .45 and fired blindly, buying seconds, and sprinted for the pier. The Zodiac waited, Spinou at the helm, engine idling.

"Move!" Raven shouted, leaping onto the boat. Spinou gunned the throttle, the Zodiac lurching as bullets slapped the water. Raven fired back, the rounds catching a gunman's chest. The shipyard shrank behind them, its cranes fading into the night.

Blood seeped from his thigh, but the flash drive was secure. Spinou's silence as he steered felt heavy. Raven's grip tightened on his pistol. The Black Sea stretched ahead, but safety was an illusion. This wasn't over.

THE ZODIAC CUT through the Black Sea's inky waves, its engine a low growl as Raven and Spinou approached a small, isolated dock. The pier jutted out like a broken finger, lined with weathered planks and illuminated by a single, flickering streetlight casting long shadows. Quiet waves lapped at the pilings, their rhythm too gentle, too lulling. Raven's kept his guard up, his wounded thigh throbbing but his senses sharp.

As Spinou tied the boat to the dock, Raven caught the Greek's hand lingering near the pistol at his hip. A subtle tell, but enough. Spinou's eyes, usually mocking, were guarded, his jaw tight. Raven's grip tightened on his own weapon, holstered but ready. The dock seemed a haven, but Raven knew better. Safehouses and quiet piers were where ops went to die. He scanned the surroundings: a cluster of rusted barrels, a stack of crates, a narrow road leading to a battered Jeep parked under a sagging warehouse. The Jeep was their exfil, but getting there felt like crossing a minefield.

"Nice work back there," Spinou said, his voice smooth but forced, as he stepped onto the dock.

Raven didn't reply, his eyes tracking Spinou's movements. The Greek's casual tone didn't match the tension in his shoulders, the way his fingers twitched toward his gun. Raven's gut screamed betrayal, but he needed proof before acting. "Let's move," he said, his voice flat, stepping onto the pier. His boots thudded softly, the only sound besides the waves.

Spinou nodded, but as they reached the crates, he raised a hand. A sharp, deliberate signal. Shadows erupted from the warehouse, four men armed with suppressed rifles, their movements swift and coordinated. Raven's fury surged, a molten wave burning away doubt. Spinou had played him, sold him out. He had to have been with the Russians back at the dock. How else would one of them have known his name? The Greek spun, drawing his pistol, a smirk curling his lips. "Hand over the drive," he taunted, "and maybe you walk."

Raven's response was a blur of motion. He dove behind a

crate, bullets splintering the wood as he drew his pistol. His anger was tempered by grim determination. This wasn't his first betrayal, and it wouldn't be his last. The flash drive, tucked in his jacket's hidden pocket, was Antonov's legacy, and he'd be damned if Spinou's men would get it. The dock's layout flashed in his mind: barrels to his left, the streetlight overhead, the Jeep fifty yards away. He could use it all.

The first gunman rounded the crate, rifle raised. Raven fired twice, the rounds punching through the man's chest. As the body fell, Raven grabbed a loose plank from the crate and hurled it at the streetlight. The bulb shattered, plunging the dock into darkness, the only light now the faint glow of the city beyond. Spinou's men hesitated, their night vision disrupted. Raven didn't. He rolled to the barrels and took out a second gunman with a headshot.

Spinou cursed, firing blindly, his rounds sparking off the barrels. Raven moved silently, slipping into the shadows between crates. The third gunman crept forward, unaware of Raven's position. Raven shot him. Blood sprayed, warm and coppery, as the body collapsed.

The fourth gunman was smarter, staying back, his rifle sweeping the darkness. Raven grabbed a rusted bolt from the ground and tossed it toward the pier's edge. The clatter drew the gunman's fire, exposing his position. Raven fired, the bullet finding the man's skull. Four down. Only Spinou remained.

Raven stalked forward, his boots silent on the damp planks. Spinou was near the Jeep, his silhouette tense, gun raised. Raven's mind flickered to interrogation, but hesitation was a luxury he couldn't afford. Spinou had betrayed Antonov, betrayed Oscar, betrayed him. The Greek's fate was sealed.

"Last chance, Spinou," Raven called, his voice low, baiting. "Drop the gun."

Spinou laughed, but it was hollow. "You think you're untouchable?" Raven put away his gun and grabbed his boot knife. This kill would be up close and personal. He charged, closing the distance before Spinou could adjust. He tackled the Greek, slamming him against the Jeep's hood. Spinou's pistol skittered away, and his fist swung, catching Raven's jaw. Pain flared, but Raven drove his knee into Spinou's gut, doubling him over. His knife flashed, sinking into Spinou's chest. The Greek gasped, eyes wide, then slumped, blood pooling beneath him.

Raven stepped back, breathing hard. He checked Spinou's body, finding nothing but a burner phone and a pack of cigarettes. No answers, only more questions. He retrieved the flash drive from his pocket, inspecting it under the Jeep's dim interior light. The casing was scratched but intact, its data—Antonov's sacrifice—still secure. Raven's thoughts turned to trust, its cost. Oscar had vouched for Spinou, and the old man's mistake had nearly killed him.

He climbed into the Jeep, its engine coughing to life, the seats worn and smelling of stale tobacco. The bodies lay scattered behind him. Raven's hands gripped the wheel, his resolve hardening. The flash drive held intel Oscar deemed important, or important enough for somebody to pay big to have it instead of somebody else. He'd deliver it to Oscar as promised, no matter who else stood in his way.

As the Jeep rumbled down the narrow road, the dock's shadows faded, swallowed by the night. Raven's eyes stayed fixed ahead, the weight of the drive in his pocket a reminder of the blood it had cost. The Black Sea stretched to his left, its waves whispering secrets he couldn't yet hear. For now, he drove, a lone figure against the dark.

THE SAFEHOUSE WAS a cramped and dimly lit apartment, its walls stained with more than age. A single bulb flickered above a scarred table with a half-empty bottle of vodka. It was a temporary refuge mirroring Raven's transient life. He sat on a creaking chair, his wounds bandaged but still aching. Across from him, Oscar sat still drinking from his glass, his weathered face etched with fatigue but sharp with focus.

Raven slid the flash drive across the table, its scratched casing a silent testament to the night's cost. "Spinou betrayed us. Whoever else wanted this—they were Russians—were waiting," he said, his voice terse, each word clipped.

Oscar's eyes darkened, guilt flickering as he picked up the drive. "I misjudged him. I'm sorry, Sam."

"I expect better from you."

Oscar met Raven's eyes for a moment. "Do you want me to grovel? I told you I was sorry."

Raven sighed and waved him off. He refilled his glass and swallowed a mouthful of vodka. Yelling at Oscar wasn't going to solve anything. Bad apples turned up sometimes.

Oscar examined the drive over, his voice steadying. "This intel—it's gold. Antonov's data exposes Russian big shots funneling arms to half the Middle East. We're talking names, routes, bank accounts. It'll save lives."

"It better save a lot," Raven said. Frustration simmered beneath his calm. He pulled his knife from its sheath, the blade still flecked with Spinou's blood. He found a rag and wet it with vodka. He cleaned the blade slowly, methodically. The steel gleamed under the bulb.

Oscar slid an envelope toward him, thick with cash. "A bonus. You earned it."

Raven pushed it back. "Keep it."

Oscar sighed, pocketing the envelope. "You're stubborn as hell, Sam. At least stay and get some rest."

Before Raven could respond, a cell phone sitting on the

table—Raven's—chimed. The screen flashed a single message: *I need you in London.* —*Ana.* Raven's pulse quickened. Ana Gray, millionaire British socialist, ran her own spy network on the side. For *fun.* And sometimes she helped western intelligence agencies catch problems they missed. She was smart but dangerous. Her SOS was cryptic, urgent, a flare in the dark. Whenever she called, it meant trouble. Raven's instinct screamed to move, to call her, but exhaustion gnawed at him, his wounds a dull roar.

"Sam, don't," Oscar said, reading his expression. "Let someone else handle it. Ana's tough. She'll hold."

Raven met his gaze, unwavering. "She wouldn't call unless it was bad. I'm going." Ana's role in his life was a shadow, but he couldn't ignore her message.

Oscar shook his head but didn't argue. He knew Raven's stubborn streak, the drive keeping him on the move when others would break.

Raven's life was a series of missions, each one bleeding into the next. To stop, to rest, was to surrender, and Raven didn't know how to surrender.

"I'll call when I'm clear," he said, his voice low but firm. Oscar nodded, a silent acknowledgment to the man who'd never stop running toward the fire. The mission never ended. Only the battlegrounds changed.

1

JUMPING OUT OF A PERFECTLY GOOD AIRPLANE PROVIDED SAM Raven his last moment of tranquility for days to come.

The Albanian Forest, 5,000 feet below, seemed peaceful, but held dangers one only saw up close. He'd be close enough to see it all soon enough. He fell through space, arms and legs extended, the thunder of rushing wind in his ears. The fall kept him from thinking about what he'd find down there. For a short period of time, he felt the freedom of birds. Nothing on the ground could touch him. He was free. For a moment, nothing mattered, not the past, the future, not the present. He wondered if death offered a similar sensation—for a microsecond. And then his mind snapped back to business.

His free fall continued for 2,000 feet, and Raven pulled the ripcord and let the parachute billow out from his back. The deployed chute yanked him with a sudden jerk, but then his fall slowed to fifteen miles per hour. It was better than the stomach-lurching 120 miles per hour of his initial descent. He was still an out-of-control body mass heading for immovable earth, moving faster than he wanted. Ravne grabbed the risers on either side and steered his fall. He wanted to land in a small opening between a cluster of trees. As he drifted closer to the ground, he made fine adjustments to make sure he stayed on target. This was no time to get stuck in a tree.

Raven touched down as gracefully as possible. He landed hard, grunting as the jolt of impact rattled every bone in his body. He followed with a tuck and roll only to end up tangled in the parachute. *Graceful, my ass.* Raven climbed out from under the silk, released his pack, and gathered up the parachute. He had to repack and bury the evidence. There was only one way out for him and his VIP, and the exit route didn't involve flying. He, of course, had to keep his VIP alive long enough to escape with him. And he had to make sure he survived the rescue, too. There were too many variables, but Raven knew how to compartmentalize. Deal with each problem as it appeared. He had a variety of experiences in the hell grounds of the world. Adapting to new battlefields wasn't difficult.

War shaped Sam Raven. He'd once worn the uniform of the 82nd Airborne, then the 5th Special Forces Group. Later, he left the military for the CIA's Ground Branch, where only a few knew the truth of his missions, and operatives shielded their identities. Now, he answered to no one. No uniform. No flag. Just a man built for battle.

Raven hadn't wanted this path. He had seen enough bloodshed to last a lifetime and tried to carve out a quiet existence. But fate had other plans. Tragedy ripped through his world, leaving only vengeance in its wake. The only reminder of his past was the silver locket he wore, its contents a secret he never shared. It was his burden—and his drive. Now, he hunted those who preyed on the innocent, turning their cruelty back on them. Justice, in his hands, came swift and final.

Raven ran for the cover of the trees. His boots crushed dried leaves into the soft dirt. Once concealed, he dropped to his knees and opened a second pack, one carried around his waist. Inside, his weapons. He removed each one, along with associated combat gear. Raven strapped a pistol to his hip and secured a combat harness across his chest. To the harness, he added spare magazines and grenades. Last, he locked a magazine into his Uzi submachine gun. The Israeli SMG and its attached suppressor would serve as head weapon. If he found something better along the way, he'd be happy to upgrade. But the potent 9mm sub gun would do the job required.

He stayed where he was to catch his breath and listen. He wanted to adjust to the new environment before proceeding and also needed to know if anybody had seen the landing. He didn't want a farmer or resident of a nearby village to wander out to see the man who fell from the sky. Trouble with civilians was a no-no, especially if the enemy paid them to sound the alarm of potential intruders. Raven was up against an organized force; one backed by the military hardware only billions in drug money provided. They worked in the Balkans and carried out their reign of terror no matter who stood in their way. Those who'd tried to stop them in the past hadn't survived.

But Raven had an edge.

He was as ruthless as the enemy.

He was in Albania, and nothing around him looked like any forest back in the US. A sea of dark green surrounded him, the thickness of the trees swallowing each other. The mass created the illusion of impenetrability. Towering beech and fir trees shaped a canopy of green overhead, muting the sun. Through gaps here and there, snow-capped mountain peaks remained visible. Shifting patterns of light broke through despite the natural resistance. It was cold, but the air was crisp and carried with it the strong scent of damp earth and pine. Somewhere, a stream trickled. Raven wanted to find the water and use it as a map reference point. He started toward the sound. The forest pressed in on him as his combat boots dug into the earth with each step. Pushing foliage out of his way, stepping over twisted tree roots, ducking under low-hanging branches, Raven made slow progress. There were far too many obstacles to trip over. A broken ankle would do him no favors. He saw no signs of human travel, only evidence of animals tracing the path. It was good and bad. Good because the likelihood of somebody finding him while on a hike was low. Bad because his biggest threat in the meantime might come from an animal that found him instead. He kept his Uzi at the ready and stopped every few steps to watch and listen. The sound of the stream grew louder.

Presently he reached the stream. The clear water flowed over a riverbed with planks of granite emerging from the earth. He could cross the water on the planks, but he wasn't sure he was going in that direction. Sitting on soft ground, Raven unfolded a map from his combat vest pocket. He used a compass on his left wrist to orient the map. North needed to be north, south to the south, all of it would have been familiar to an experienced hiker...or special operator on a black mission. Raven was off the books. No government, especially the USA, had sent him into the Albanian wilderness. He was there as a favor to an old friend. An SOS is an SOS and he couldn't turn away.

He plotted his march using the map, from his position at the stream, to where he knew the target compound to be. He'd landed in the right spot. He was only three miles east of the goal. An easy march if he took it slow. He timed it out. He'd be there by nightfall unless a bear ate him along the way. *Note to self, avoid bears.* Raven refolded the map and tucked it away. Using the compass again, he found his bearings and started off. He was marching into danger once again and doing so in a region where one easily vanished. If he didn't get out of Albania alive, nobody would ever find a trace of him.

———————

THE MISSION WAS rescue and recovery.

Ana Gray, a rich British socialite, ran her own private spy network using a variety of assets. She sold information to interested governments and advised on threats to their national security. Often, regardless if she had official permission or not, Ana directed hired commandos at threats when bureaucratic red tape became too thick. The intelligence community tolerated her. She enjoyed the "me vs. them" aspect.

Ana's SOS made Raven hurry to London to discover the extent of the new crisis. He'd arrived three days before his parachute jump, and they talked over coffee and tea on her balcony. The wide balcony covered the length of the exterior wall. The marble railing overlooked a lush green pasture. Birds chirped. It was nice to be away from the city. Like Raven, Ana Gray enjoyed quiet.

"What do you know about the Balkan Cartel?" she said.

Ana Gray sat with her dark hair pulled back, a fitted white blouse hugging her frame like a corset. The blouse emphasized what little she had up top. Black Capris sat low on her hips. To Raven, they only highlighted her thin legs—she walked on toothpicks. Still, she was worth billions, not unattractive otherwise, and often appeared on the world's most eligible bachelorette lists. A diamond necklace adorned her slender neck. She was never without an example of her expensive jewelry collection.

She and Raven had worked together several times in the past.

Raven answered her question.

"It stretches from Turkey through Albania, Montenegro, Serbia and Bosnia. I can't remember the name of the fellow who runs the show."

"Doesn't matter. He's dead."

"Oh."

"Plane crash. But it wasn't an accident."

"Engineered?"

"It's the running theory."

"He was removed because—"

"The new boss wanted to take over."

"And who is the new boss?"

"Nobody knows," Ana said.

"Great. Want me to discover who he is?"

"I sent somebody to find out, but she's been captured, and I need you to go and get her. She's at a compound in Albania, where cartel troops take prisoners to torture them until they crack. They have all kinds of military goodies, Raven. Small arms, vehicles. The forest is their playground."

"Why is discovering the new leader so important?"

"Because the cartel," Ana said, "is preparing to release a new synthetic opioid called Black Ember. They want to target Western Europe."

Raven sipped his tea. Yeah, always a sucker. Another dive into hell. Such was his war without end.

"I'll start as soon as my fee is in my account."

"Have I ever cheated you?"

Raven grinned over the rim of his mug.

"What's the asset's name?" he asked.

"Elena Covaci. One of my undercover specialists. I don't know how she got captured, but she's in danger."

"She could expose your entire organization."

"It's a risk, sure."

"She may be dead already."

"My sources say she isn't. At least as of today."

"I'll find her," Raven said. "And if I find out she didn't make it?"

Ana shrugged. "I'll regroup and try again."

Typical Ana, Raven thought. He swallowed more of his tea.

2

RAVEN FELT ALONE IN A NEST FULL OF VIPERS.

The pictures of the target compound hadn't communicated its size. What Raven observed from a high perch would have scared off any but the most dedicated soldier. To Raven, the scale came in handy. It was difficult to contain small problems within a large base. He could be out and away with Elena Covaci before a major response formed.

The compound sat within clusters of towering pines. High chain-link fence, electrified. Topped with razor wire, too—overkill didn't hurt anybody but the intruders you wanted to keep out. Prefabricated structures filled the compound. Quonset huts for barracks. A few wood buildings, their camo-painted walls and crude roofs showing hasty production. Associated dishes and antennas sat atop the roof of a wooden structure at the center of the compound.

The barracks occupied the east side of the compound. Near the metal huts was a fenced-in square area for heavy-duty trucks. A few of the trucks had canvas covers over the back; the others remained exposed.

Guard towers at each corner, four total. The towers were open, no glass enclosing the post. Each tower sported a swivel-mounted heavy machine gun.

Ana Gray's intel suggested fifty to seventy-five men stationed within. They had one responsibility other than combat training. They needed to guard the brick building on the west side. A building with no windows. The brick building was a cartel prison, and the camp a place to extract information via torture. The forest was a place to dispose of the bodies. Raven had to make sure Elena's body didn't get buried in the wilderness.

He left his position and moved east over the rough terrain. His next hiding spot offered a view of the main gate. It was a fence swinging inward, opened and closed by one of the two guards who rotated the position. Between the gate and the trucks sat the double rows of Quonset barracks. Elena was on the west end, trucks on the east, and a long run in between. She may or may not be in shape to handle such a physical extreme. Raven had no idea of her present condition. He only knew she was still there, and still alive, because of the guards at the brick building. The odds were against him and his VIP, but he'd faced the impossible before.

Raven left his hiding spot and proceeded south, away from the compound. He needed to rest for a while. He'd be busy after midnight.

THREE DAYS.

Sitting in the dark for three days.

Surely, David Jocic thought, *she's softened up by now.*

Jocic oversaw the compound as its highest-ranking officer. He wasn't sure if the posting was a reward for good service or punishment for an unknown infraction. With his old boss dead, and a new leader in place, Jocic had appealed for a new assignment. So far, his request had been ignored. He remained at the compound and made the best of it. One did not argue with The Wolf. One did as ordered or faced the consequences.

Jocic was a member of the Balkan Cartel. Drugs, weapons, human trafficking. The Balkan Cartel had fingers in every pie, and The Wolf sat atop the empire on a metaphorical throne of gold. The organization covered more of the Balkan region than any other crime syndicate.

Jocic started small in the organization. He had dreams of being much more than a glorified prison guard, but here he was.

Jocic walked across the compound. He wore camo green like his men. Unlike his men, he was not armed. His troops stood at their posts with weapons, and he didn't think he needed to keep a gun handy. They were in the middle of nowhere. Who would attack them? His men may have disliked being far from civilization, but they knew who was in charge. They feared The Wolf the same as Jocic. Failure to carry out assigned duties only ended badly.

The two guards at the brick building snapped to attention as he approached. His was a disciplined force, for sure. All carried the latest Kalashnikov rifles. They were ready for a war, should a war ever break out in the armpit of the Albanian forest.

Jocic greeted the guards and one produced a ring of keys to unlock the door. The other handed him a flashlight.

The door squeaked open.

Jocic turned on the flashlight and stepped inside.

JOCIC HAD to give credit to the builders of the prison—they did a good job. No leaks, no drafts, no windows. Pitch black only. Multiple cells, but only one occupied at present. Jocic shined the light down the narrow corridor with the barred cells on either side. He heard the woman breathing, and it sounded like labored breathing. He reached the end of the aisle and aimed the light through the bars. The smell hit his nose first. Then the sight of Elena Covaci sitting in a corner, her clothes soiled, her hair a tangled mess. She moved her hair out of her face and started into the flashlight.

"It's been three days," Jocic said.

She stared at him.

"Feel like talking?"

Elena made an animal sound deep in her throat. She didn't open her mouth.

"We can let you die here," Jocic said.

Finally, Elena spoke.

"No, you won't," she said.

She sounded hoarse.

Jocic laughed. "Don't think you're so important we won't let you die."

"You want to know…who sent me."

Now Jocic had no reply.

Elena continued. As she spoke, she put more strength behind her voice. "You want to know who will come after I'm gone."

"Perhaps your successor won't make the same mistake you did, Elena."

She laughed. "You think it was a mistake?"

"Being thrown in here on purpose doesn't seem like a good strategy, Elena. It will earn you nothing but a hole in the ground. I'll try not to throw your body on top of anybody else we buried out there."

Elena tried to spit at him, but nothing came out.

It's the thought that counts, he decided.

"We will continue our chat shortly," he said. "I'll have you hosed off and we'll give you a little food. Then the questioning begins again."

"I won't answer."

"Then the beating begins, Elena. I'll show you how good I am with a paddle and whip. Or maybe only the whip."

He departed, shining the light ahead, walking with eager anticipation. He wondered if The Wolf left him in the forest because of his hobby of torturing people...

3

THE GUARD LET HER EAT THE HALF BOWL OF SOUP AND PIECE of black bread before dragging her outside.

The guard tossed her to Jocic, who grabbed her by both arms and tossed her to two more troopers. The pair pulled and ripped at what remained of Elena's clothes and left her naked and barefoot. They finished the humiliation by zip-tying her hands behind her back. Jocic turned on a hose. Elena screamed as the hard spray of cold water struck her. The force of the blast knocked her over, and she fell. Jocic focused the spray on her face, then the dirt. She was rolling in the mud, trying to get back on her feet. Finally, she stopped trying and lay there. The water blast stopped. Two troopers picked her up and set her on her feet. Jocic hosed off the mud. When he shut off the water, she stood shivering, dripping. Elena looked around, turning her head and body to take in the sight. A circle of men surrounded her. Lights shined. There was nowhere to run. If she tried to breach the wall of men, they'd toss her back into the center of the circle.

The scene around her was a kaleidoscope of images she tried to process. Stripped nude in front of a bunch of luring creeps wasn't important. She needed mental notes on the compound to take back to Ana Gray. The section of her mind concerned with survival kicked in to try and reach her original goal. The alternative meant panic, and panic wasn't going to get her anywhere.

Her eyes searched the darkness beyond the lights and the circle of men. She was looking for hope. Some sign Ana Gray hadn't abandoned her. But her vision was blurry, and she didn't discern any of the hope she wanted to find. All she saw was a black void, and if her situation didn't change, the void was where she was heading.

Then Jocic stepped up to her and showed off his whip.

RAVEN DUG. His USGI shovel broke the surface of the soft dirt without difficulty, and he dumped the piles off to the side. He didn't have to dig far. The supply case buried by Ana's scout team showed itself within a few minutes. He pulled it from the hole and brushed it off. Using a key Ana had given him, he unlocked the case and raised the lid.

The night's chill wasn't enough to keep him from sweating. He worked fast, bringing out the satchel within the wooden crate and setting it on the ground. He pulled out a bundle of women's clothes—jeans, a sweater, a pair of tennis shoes. The satchel also contained C-4 plastic explosive and remote detonators. Raven packed the C-4 in his rucksack, adding the clothes for Elena, too.

He made the return march north using night-vision goggles. He stopped every few minutes to listen to the environment and scan the dark with his natural vision. Still no sign of cartel patrols, and no sign of bears or other dangerous animals. He didn't hear any small critters, either. They must have been hiding. But he kept the Uzi at the ready, the suppressor on the muzzle extending the barrel length. It wasn't easy moving in the dark, but he pressed on. Elena Covaci was waiting.

The hoots and hollers and glare of bright lights reached him before he arrived at the perimeter. He didn't have to work too hard to hide this time. All camp personnel seemed to be in the open area near the brick prison. When he saw the object of their attention, a chill from more than the night's temperature raced down his back. A man with a whip attacked a naked woman with her arms tied behind her. She shuffled on muddy ground, trying to avoid the impact of the whip. When she fell, two men stood her up again, and the man with the whip continued. They weren't bothering to question her. It was a torture show.

He had to hurry.

Raven went to work with the C-4 charges and detonators. The lights and distractions were perfect. The brightness ruined any night vision the soldiers had and allowed Raven to hide in the shadows. He mined each guard tower, then planted a charge at the western fence near the commotion and the prison.

He was breathing hard, trying not to rush, forcing himself to pause and go slow so as not to make a mistake. Any mistake spelled doom for him and Elena. He didn't want to waste the opportunity handed to him, but every time she screamed...

With the last of the charges rigged, Raven considered an escape option he'd pondered since his recon. A dirt road led from the compound's main gate. Raven wasn't sure where the road led, but a road was a road. If he could get his hands on one of the trucks, he might be able to find out where the road went.

The whip cracked. Elena cried out. The men cheered. Another man began yelling over the commotion, as if he were asking questions at the same time. The man's voice echoed, but Raven blocked out the words. He was falling back to a safe spot. When he touched off the C-4, he'd unleash a hellstorm the likes of which the cartel soldiers had never seen. Or would ever see again.

JOCIC LIKED HIS WHIP. He liked to use it on prisoners because of the fear the little handheld blacksnake inspired. He knew how to wield it for greatest effect. The tip didn't need to touch the subject or even break skin. The shock of the *crack* and the illusion of impact elicited cries of terror from the most stoic subjects. Elena Covaci wasn't immune to the illusion either. Her dark eyes widened every time he drew back his arm. Her scream every time the tip came within millimeters of her pale white body made his men cheer. He managed to score a few hits; the bloody marks on her body testified to his accuracy.

He raised the whip again, then lowered his arm and laughed at the wave of relief on her face. He stepped close so she could hear him speak over the noise of his men.

"Tell me what I want to know and this stops. Who sent you?"

This time, she managed to spit at him.

His men booed. They yelled for him to whip her again.

"I'm going to peel the flesh from your body, Elena. You'll beg to tell me everything by the time I'm done."

"Shut up and do it!"

Jocic took two steps back and raised his arm.

4

NOBODY NOTICED THE FLASHES OF THE C-4 CHARGES RIGHT away. The bright lights focused on Elena Covaci tricked everyone's eyesight. The cartel troopers didn't know what was happening until the explosions took on power. The blasts were thunderclaps in the forest. They brought light to pitch black and fire where it was free to consume and destroy with unlimited fuel. The ground shook with each blast, and then the first of the guard towers tipped over. The legs holding up the platform buckled, and the tower fell like a tree. It tipped away from the compound, crashing through branches and leaves. The tower then stopped, tangled in the trees, but the men within the shack atop kept falling. They screamed until they struck the ground. More explosions rocked the compound. A billow of flame assaulted the base of the remaining towers. The fence on the west end erupted in a ball of fire. The blast tore a chunk of dirt out of the ground and flung the chain-link in all directions. The barracks on the east side vanished in a flash. One thunderous explosion after another, bringing heat, flames, the scent of roasting flesh.

Jocic didn't need to shout orders. His men were ready to fight. They clutched Kalashnikov rifles and looked for the source of the incoming threat. The rest ran in search of equipment to fight the fire. They had to run through the flames and dodge burning debris as it fell to the ground.

Jocic dropped his whip and left Elena Covaci lying in the puddle of mud. He ran to the building in the center of the compound where his office was. He had his weapons there. The crew inside would be on the radio, trying to alert other cartel forces in the area to their problem. The priority was pushing back the attacking force, whoever they were. Then, evacuation. There would be no saving the compound. Nor the forest surrounding it. Jocic had no idea how bad the resulting inferno would be, but he had no intention of being around to find out.

The bright flames, the heat, the choking cloud of smoke all around him—it made running hard, seeing difficult, and thinking even tougher. And then Jocic realized he didn't hear any shooting. No shooting from his men, for sure, but also no shooting from anybody else. No strike force raiding the compound. What the hell was going on? It was the last thought Jocic had before he saw, and then heard, the big truck barreling through the compound.

RAVEN DROVE one of the trucks out of the motor pool before touching off another C-4 charge. He found the truck parked with the key in the ignition. Raven gave the key a twist and the big motor roared to life. The fires were spreading, the smoke thick. Raven kept the side windows shut and flicked the dash vents closed. He shifted into first gear and let the deuce-and-a-half roll forward.

The truck advanced into hell.

The cabin heated up right away, and smoke obscured the windshield, but he still had an advantage. The cartel troopers had nobody to shoot at. They weren't going to start shooting at one of their own trucks just because.

Behind him, the C-4 charge detonated. One of the parked deuces left the ground as the explosion billowed. It landed on a lake of fire, flaming embers flying onto other trucks. The embers brought more destruction. The blaze was running out of control fast.

One of Raven's mentors had once told him: *When all else fails, fireworks.*

Raven turned right and accelerated. Men ran out of the way. Some held portable fire extinguishers, and others manned powerful hoses. They attacked the overwhelming blazes with heavy streams of water. Other troopers, guns ready, still looking for something to shoot at, acted as human shields. Raven drove by. They didn't recognize him as an intruder, if they took notice of his face at all. To maintain the illusion, he didn't try to run them over. He needed to get to Elena before the fire reached her...

AT LEAST IT was warm now.

But Elena Covaci knew she had minutes left. And no way out. The smoke was bad enough. The flames were insult to injury. She was still on the ground, in the mud, trying to stay low while taking in the action around her. She coughed. Smoke stung her eyes. What seemed like a rescue now seemed—

The big truck rumbled toward her. Slow enough to let cartel troopers run out of the way, but approaching her still, which made no sense. Was this—no, too much to hope for. Men with hoses sprayed water at the fire, but to Elena, the fire looked like it was winning. How much water did the compound have? Surely not enough...

The truck stopped beside her. A man dressed in black, unlike anybody else in the compound, jumped out with a knife. He said the words she wanted to hear while cutting the zip tie holding her arms behind her back.

"Ana sent me! She said to tell you code yellow!"

Elena's eyes widened as the man put away his knife and then helped her stand. He shoved her in the direction of the truck. She managed to get on the sidestep and climb into the cabin, sliding across to the passenger seat. She ignored the pain of her injuries. She ignored the fact she had no clothes. What seemed unreal was real. Ana hadn't left her to die here after all.

And then Jocic reached the truck. He had a rifle now and raised the weapon to fire. The man sent by Ana kicked Jocic in the face. As the cartel torturer fell back, the man grabbed the Uzi from under his right arm. He fired short bursts, shifting his aim, driving approaching troopers to cover. Elena saw them scatter, but a few returned fire. The man climbed behind the wheel as the bullets snapped into the deuce's steel frame.

"Stay down!"

She was still naked, and the hard steel interior was cold against her skin. Elena ducked below the dash. The man spun the big truck in a wide turn. Bullets smacked the body; a few rounds punched holes in the thick glass. Sharp pieces fell on her left shoulder. *A few more cuts won't hurt.*

The truck moved faster as the man who rescued her shifted into low and ran the engine hard.

"Almost there, hang on!"

Almost where? And how did he expect her to make it through the forest without any clothes?

5

SPEED WAS FINE, BUT HE NEEDED TO SHOOT TOO.

A line of gunmen formed ahead, and Raven pressed the accelerator. He hand-cranked the window down, grabbed the Uzi with his left hand, and shoved the sub gun out. The suppressor made it tip down; he cocked his wrist to raise the muzzle and pulled the trigger. The mag emptied after a short stutter of fire, but the line scattered. Three stood their ground and fired Kalashnikov AK-203s, but they didn't stop the truck. The deuce squashed them beneath the behemoth tires with barely a bump felt in the cabin.

He pulled the Uzi back and glanced at the naked woman hiding under the dash. He smiled. Her face remained stoic. He looked forward again and decided he must have looked like he was leering at her.

"I have clothes for you, don't worry."

The woman said, "I *was* wondering."

Then came the crash.

The big truck shook as Raven plowed the front end through the main gate. He continued onto the dirt road.

Raven had figured out where the road went thanks to his map, but it didn't lead anywhere he wanted to go. But the road would take them far enough from the compound to suit his needs. The other trucks in the motor pool still burned. The cartel troopers weren't going to come after him on foot.

Raven scooted forward in his seat, holding the wheel with one hand while he slid the pack off his back. He passed it to Elena. "Jeans, shoes, sweater," he told her. He set the pack between the seats. Elena rose from under the dash and managed to dress despite the lingering mud and awkward space. She pulled the sweater over her head, wincing as the material touched her wounds. While tying her hair back, she said, "Where are we going?"

"Not far. And then I need you ready to walk."

"I'll be ready."

"I'm Sam Raven."

"Elena Covaci."

They didn't shake hands.

"What does code yellow mean?" Raven asked.

"It's a code between Ana and me. It means I won't shoot you when you turn your back."

"Happy thought."

"Thank you for getting me out of there."

"Sorry I couldn't do it sooner."

She scoffed. "I've been through worse."

"Do the clothes fit?" he asked.

"That's a stupid question," she said.

Raven was going to say more, but a glance in the side mirror stopped him.

He hadn't destroyed all the compound's vehicles after all.

A Jeep and a motorcycle were gaining fast.

"Elena?"

"What?"

He took out his pistol and handed it to her.

"You're going to need this."

BY THE TIME David Jocic made it to his feet, the truck was turning and speeding away. He started shouting commands, rallying those around him. He already knew the motor pool near the barracks was burning. Smaller vehicles waited within a second fenced-in area at the north end. None of the fires had spread there yet. Jocic and his men ran, some with difficulty because of the smoke. They reached the vehicles, US surplus jeeps and British motorcycles, within two minutes. Jocic and three others climbed into a Jeep. Two more found a Triumph motorcycle—one rider, one in the sidecar. Motors revved to life. Jocic told his driver not to waste time. The Jeep and motorcycle tore through the compound. Most of his men were still fighting the blaze, but the water would run out soon. The rest of his leadership team knew what they had to do before full evac. What they did wasn't top of Jocic's mind. He wanted the spy dead, and to murder her rescuer slowly. When they sped through the crashed gate and onto the dirt road, he checked his rifle.

And prepared to even the score his way.

"CAN YOU RUN?" Raven asked.

"I can do whatever I have to do to survive."

Raven decided she wasn't so much as answering the question as she was stating a familiar mantra.

"I need more ammo," she told him.

Raven had three spare 10-round extension magazines for

his .45 on his chest harness. He pulled them out and handed them to her. She stuffed the mags in the left pocket of her jeans. "Why a 1911?" she asked. "Haven't you ever heard of a Glock?"

"That's a stupid question," Raven said. He smiled at her. She surprised him with a smile back.

A shot cracked behind them, and the side mirror on Raven's door shattered.

"Hang on!"

Raven wrenched the wheel hard to the right, sending the big deuce off the dirt road and onto the thick forest floor. The behemoth flattened and crunched the foliage and Raven drove as far as he could before nature's mass prevented further movement.

"Out my side!" he yelled, shoving the door open. He stopped the truck at an angle off the road to cover their exit. They had seconds to put distance between them and the enemy. They didn't lack cover, but the enemy had the advantage of knowing the terrain better than them.

Raven dropped out of the cabin and readied the Uzi submachine gun with a fresh magazine. He kept the suppressor in place. If they couldn't hear him shooting in the dark, it gave him an advantage. Elena ran with him into the darkness. The enemy may have known the terrain, but they were both fighting in the dark. And Raven also had his night vision kit handy.

Raven and Elena stopped, rustled leaves as they took cover, and waited. Elena breathed harder than Raven, with little whimpers escaping her lips. The torture of the night and the last few days was catching up.

The Jeep and motorcycle took longer to arrive than Raven thought. The leader of the team jumped out and issued orders. He was smart enough to use the deuce to block the view of him and his men. Raven had no clear shots at any of them.

"Who is in charge?" he asked.

"His name is Jocic. He's mine to kill, not yours."

"I'll do my best to let you," he told her. Raven donned his night-vision goggles and waited for Jocic to make a move.

upon them.

6

JOCIC AND HIS MEN CRAWLED BENEATH THE DEUCE-AND-A-half. He listened. The normal night sounds were gone, but Jocic wanted to hear if Elena and her rescuer were moving. They were close, he knew. Ready to fight. But so was he. One of his men belly-crawled beside him. They were under the front of the deuce.

"They can't see us either," the trooper said.

"Is it only the two of them, or more?" Jocic wondered aloud. The trooper had no answer.

Jocic looked up at the deuce, then began directing. He told the two who'd arrived on the motorcycle to move left; they had fifteen seconds. At the end of fifteen seconds, he was going to turn on the truck's headlights.

"PUT YOUR HEAD DOWN," Raven whispered, and removed his NVGs. Elena, seeing the motion, kept her from asking why.

When the headlights snapped on, their vision wasn't ruined. Raven opened his eyes slowly to let them adjust. If

Jocic and his men were expecting to catch him and Elena in the open, he was disappointed.

Then Jocic gave the order to fire. The two he sent off to the left let off a couple of short bursts, probing shots. The rounds went wide. Raven grinned and lined up the Uzi's sights, switched to single shot, and fired once. The light worked for the enemy, and against them, too. Raven's shot didn't connect, deflected by natural obstacles, but it was enough to spook the gunmen. They stopped firing and scrambled to move.

Then Kalashnikov return fire erupted, the Jocic crew firing in random patterns. Raven and Elena flattened into the dirt. The rounds whistled overhead and smacked into tree trunks. The shooting stopped. Raven poked the Uzi through the foliage and fired twice. The Uzi whispered, only the action clicking as it cycled. This time he scored. One of the Jocic gunners near the deuce yelled and fell. Raven flipped to burst most and fired again. The yelling stopped.

"Cover me," Elena said.

Before Raven replied, she was on the move, rising and pivoting and exposing them both. Raven responded the only way possible. Bumping the selector switch to full auto, he let the Uzi do the talking. The submachine gun stuttered some more. Elena's fleeing figure attracted pot shots, but the enemy was keeping their head down to avoid the fusillade of 9mm death from the silent Uzi. Then the weapon clicked empty, the bolt closed, and Raven left the position to reload on the run. Enemy fire chased him, a couple of 7.62x39 rounds from the AK-203s chunking into the tree he dropped behind. Raven fired around the side, and Elena joined in with the .45 pistol. One of the deuce's headlights winked out. Jocic ordered his men forward. Raven leaned further out from the trunk and started shooting once more.

He counted six, then five. His bursts knocked one down.

The others opened fire and Raven dropped and rolled. Elena squeezed off more .45 blasts, two rapid shots; Jocic gave more orders, and the gunners spread out. Raven fired, missed, moved again. He had a clear shot at Jocic when he took aim again but held back. He was Elena's target. Raven shifted his aim and fired; another gunner down. The remaining troops spotted Elena and turned their AKs in her direction. Raven let them have it, two stuttering bursts, ripping a pattern of holes across their chests. The gunmen tumbled into the brush.

Jocic and his last trooper advanced. Raven moved to get out of the remaining headlight's glare. Only Jocic focused on Raven. The other looked for Elena. She popped up and fired once before the gunner reacted. Jocic fired at Raven, missing, then pivoted toward Elena. She shot him in the stomach; he doubled over, stifling a cry. He still had enough strength to raise his weapon. Raven covered him with the Uzi but there was no need to fire. Elena's follow-up blasts of .45 ACP power hit Jocic in the head. His body dropped with the others.

Elena reloaded the pistol as she ran back to Raven. "All right, this is a good gun."

"Good shooting, too."

"Thanks for not killing him."

"You had it under control." He slung the Uzi. She offered back the pistol, and he holstered it. "Keep the mags for now," he told her.

His boots crunched on the ground as he started for the vehicles. She caught up. "What are we taking?"

"Motorcycle is the best option."

"Let's take the sidecar off. I'll ride on the back of the seat."

Disconnecting the sidecar was as easy as lifting out two four-inch bolts. They tossed it aside. The motorcycle was an old Triumph TR6R with a 650cc engine. The cartel loved their vintage machines. Raven swung over the seat and Elena joined him, wrapping her arms around his midsection. He kicked the bike to life. The tires had good tread; navigating the terrain wouldn't be hard, and it beat the hell out of walking. He wasn't sure Elena was up to the challenge since the fight was over.

"Where to?" she asked.

"Ana set up a place for us."

He accelerated, steering around a body or two, finding a narrow path to keep the tires on. Raven liked how Elena handled herself in the fight. He hoped she wasn't badly injured. Didn't appear so. He wanted to know the truth about her mission. He wanted to see it finished. He needed Elena to fill in the blanks. *Patience*, he thought. Get to the safehouse first. Regroup. The leftover cartel troops could still come after them. There was no time to relax yet.

The Triumph rumbled as they pressed on.

THE SAFEHOUSE WAS near Lake Shkodra, close to the border of Montenegro. Lake access was via a footpath, and neighbors were few and far between. Raven parked the Triumph out front. Elena hopped off first and went to lean with both hands on the high porch rail. Like the rest of the cabin, it was a well-finished piece of timber. She was breathing hard. Raven went over but didn't touch her.

"Are you—"

"I need a minute." She clenched her teeth, stifling a wince. He saw the pain on her face.

"There's a shower and a medical kit inside."

"Okay, get the door open."

Raven unlocked the door with a heavy-duty key, and she followed him inside.

Raven checked the interior. He ignored the basic furniture. Like the crate of C-4, other Ana Gray operatives prepared the cabin in advance of Raven's arrival. He found the bedrooms. One contained a suitcase of women's clothes. Elena didn't bother with it; she found the first aid kit in the bathroom, shut the door, and left Raven alone.

He kept the Uzi slung crossbody and stood outside in the dark. The night sounds returned. Critters. Nocturnal variety. None who walked on two legs. He checked the perimeter. No close neighbors, as Ana told him, and a rippling lake. He went back inside and locked the door. Time to settle down for a bit. He heard the water running in the shower, but also heard Elena crying. He went back outside to check the perimeter again.

7

ELENA EXITED THE BATHROOM WRAPPED IN A TOWEL AND
closed the door to her bedroom. Raven returned from
outside and went to the kitchen to prepare a pot of tea. A
small selection waited in one of the cupboards; he scowled at
most of it. There was a lot of flavored tea. Flavored tea was
"girl tea" but he finally found a few packs of English Breakfast. He wondered if Elena wanted any, so he opened three
packs, filled the kettle, and waited for the water to boil. After
taking it off the burner, he placed the packs inside to steep.

Elena came out of her bedroom in the new clothes from
the suitcase. She stopped to look around the room as if it was
her first time seeing the layout.

"Feel like some tea?"

"I didn't use all the hot water," she said instead, then
continued. "I messed up, okay? That's why you had to come
get me."

"I didn't ask."

She joined him in the kitchen and said she'd like tea,
please. "How did you find me?"

Raven poured two mugs and handed one to her. He

needed a shower, too. He wanted out of the combat rig in a hurry. The fabric of his black suit clung to his sweaty skin, and stank of gunpowder and motorcycle fumes.

"Ana reached me when it was evident you'd gone missing," he said. "She feared the worst, but you apparently have friends in low places. They provided the compound location, and I jumped out of a perfectly good airplane."

"You fell from the sky like my guardian angel?"

"Hardly. I don't feel like an angel."

———

RAVEN SET up a laptop on the dining table the next morning after clearing off his breakfast dishes. He left food in the frying pan on the stove for Elena—if she ever rolled out of bed. It was time to call Ana Gray and tell her the results.

When Ana's face filled the monitor, she didn't waste time with preamble.

"Success?"

"I got her," Raven reported.

"You look tired."

"Still waking up."

"Where is she?"

"Zonked. When I found her—"

"I don't want to know. The point is you got her out and we can continue."

Raven turned his head as Elena emerged from her bedroom in a white bathrobe. Her hair dangled in an unruly fashion. She pulled another chair from the table and sat beside him.

"Ana?" she said.

"You hurt bad?"

"Been through worse."

"Tell me what happened," Ana said.

"I screwed up. Vercuni's wife caught me snooping."

"Did you confirm—"

"I confirmed nothing, Ana. We're nowhere closer to the new leader's identity than we were when I started."

"Okay. Go wash your face, sweetie. Raven, we need to talk some more."

"I'm still here." He watched the screen while Elena departed.

"Is she gone?"

"Yes."

"All right. I sent Elena because the new leader of the Balkan Cartel may be the man who murdered her family during the Yugoslav War."

Raven shook his head.

"What?"

"You always know how to exploit somebody's motivation, Ana."

"It gets the job done, Raven. Now listen. The man we suspect is the new leader is General Dragoslav Nikolic. Not only do we need to stop him from releasing the new synthetic opioid, but we need to deliver him to The Hague. He's still a wanted war criminal."

"Why didn't you tell me this when we started?"

"You didn't need to know then. Come on, Raven. You know how I work."

Raven sighed. "What do you want done?"

"Elena will provide more detail. For now, focus on the cartel. I want it gone, Raven. If you discover CIA fingerprints, do what you think is best."

"All right," Raven said. "One smashed cartel coming right up."

"In exchange for another fee."

"I won't refuse," he said.

"On the way. Now listen. Our main contact is in

Montenegro. She's a journalist named Irina Vukovic. You can trust her—she cultivated my other sources and has published a lot about the cartel for her newspaper. She's sort of an expert."

"Sort of."

"I said you can trust her."

"I believe you," Raven said.

"And she may have a target on her back," Ana pointed out.

"Don't we all."

"I don't." She smiled.

"Are you sure?" He didn't smile.

"Good luck, Raven. Keep me posted."

"Yeah." Raven ended the video call and the screen returned to the desktop display. He looked across the room. Elena's bedroom door remained closed. He wondered if she heard any of the conversation.

PODGORICA, Montenegro. The nation's capital, sometimes called "the most boring capital in Europe," but not by looking at it. Surrounded by green hills, the city looked like an artist's color palette when viewed from one of those hills. White buildings, a lot of green from trees, red roof faded to pink from the sun. Podgorica had a lot of color and the building exteriors reflected the overall element of the city. Podgorica might not be as famous as Paris, but it was sure as hell nicer.

But there were parts of the city Irina Vukovic didn't think were very nice at all.

She steered her compact car along a rough road which needed repaving thirty years ago and had only deteriorated to a worse state since. She drove slowly to not only avoid the bumps and potholes and cracks but also look for a specific address. She was twenty miles outside the city, where rundown buildings dominated, with some concealed by big trees adjacent or in front of the structures. Modern Podgorica development hadn't reached this far and Irina would have preferred being anywhere else, but she was a reporter, and a good one, and getting the story often meant traveling into unpleasant areas, either in town or other parts of the globe. She'd done it all in her fifteen-year career.

Another bump. Her coffee spilled in the center cup holder. She cursed. Keeping her car clean was part of Irina's regular routine. She spent a lot of time in the car and didn't want it dirty. It was also how she avoided the stereotype of the sloppy reporter. Too many of her colleagues left their cars messy. Too many wore their clothes wrinkled and maintained an unkempt appearance because they thought it was cool. Irina didn't sport designer clothes or carry an expensive purse or wear shoes costing twice her salary, but she liked to dress nicely, if not checking all the "business casual" boxes. Her long dark hair and dark eyes were her most prominent features, though most noticed her perpetual frown first. Friends and colleagues and family were always accusing her of being grumpy or unhappy. It wasn't her fault; it was her Resting Bitch Face.

Her current assignment related to discovering the name of the new leader of the Balkan Cartel. The shakeup following the death of the previous boss was still reverberating through the halls of Montenegro law enforcement. The other Balkan territories also had a vested interest in the new man's name. She was meeting a source who allegedly had the man's name and knew how he'd orchestrated his rise to power. Irina wasn't sure exposing the new leader would lead to a renewed effort on the part of law enforcement, but it would for sure rob the new boss of the mystery and let the region know who to blame for the increased drug flow. A flow bringing only death and destruction and ruining lives.

She was setting herself up for a murder attempt by writing the story, but she'd been carrying a target on her back for most of her career. One more wasn't going to hurt.

And exposing the cartel kingpin was worth the risk. As much as she tried not to be a righteous crusader, sometimes Irina embraced the role.

She finally stopped at a cluster of mobile homes and found an empty parking spot in a section for guests. The resident must not have expected many guests, because there were only three spaces. She was the only driver making use of one. Grabbing her purse from the passenger seat, Irina exited her car.

The homes were like the rest of the neighborhood, old, paint fading, in need of more than a facelift. But the residents made an effort to keep everything neat and tidy, and she appreciated the work. Nothing was too messy; gardens aplenty; a black cat crossed the roadway in front of her, and she laughed at the thought of the feline being a bad omen. She walked and noted address numbers until she found a unit in fading blue marked 1953. Up a narrow set of steps to the door. Quick knock. When she knocked, the door opened. It stopped after moving inward half an inch.

Maybe the black cat...

Oh, you gotta be kidding...

"Luka?"

She pushed the door open further. The hinges squeaked. She didn't step inside.

"Luka, it's Irina, from the newspaper."

No response. Irina returned to her car and dialed the police on her cell. Let them figure out what was going on inside. Because if the worst had happened, and Luka was dead, it meant she was on the right track. It also meant the cartel wanted to keep their secret. Which meant her source wasn't going to be the last to die.

8

IRINA WAS SITTING IN HER CAR WHEN THE POLICE ARRIVED. SHE watched them in the car's mirrors. The first officers stopped their car in front of Luka's mobile unit and spent three minutes inside before they emerged with grim expressions. One put a strip of yellow crime scene tape across the open door. The other took a moment to get on the radio and call in their discovery. Irina's heart sank. Luka was dead for sure. She wanted to wait until the homicide detectives showed up. She didn't know the beat cops and they didn't know her. They'd only tell her to wait for the detectives anyway to give her statement. The two cops stood outside and unit and waited. Same as she.

Thirty minutes later, more officials arrived. The crime scene crew, the coroner. No detectives. Finally, a dark blue sedan drove up. A robust balding man in a frumpy suit emerged from the car. He looked around. Irina left the car and hurried across the pavement.

"Stojanovic! Lieutenant Stojanovic!"

The stocky man turned. He was shorter than her, with a fat face and big cheeks.

"What are you doing here?"

"You're here because I called," she said.

"Did you go inside?"

"Are you kidding?"

Stojanovic looked at her with a stoic expression. He waited for more, but Irina wasn't going to volunteer information until he asked. She knew him from previous stories she'd covered, and they respected each other. He wasn't as combative as some of his colleagues, but he didn't have any more love for newspaper reporters than they did.

"I still need an answer to my first question, Irina."

"I'm on assignment. Luka—the victim—was my source."

"A source for—"

"It's a Balkan Cartel story."

"Ah ha. Luka who? What was his last name?"

She told him.

"And why was he a source?"

"He was a low-level member."

"Talking to you because?"

"I'm trying to—you know. Expose the new boss."

"Ah ha. Everybody wants to know who the new boss is. Every fink on the street is asking for favors because they tell us they know who the new boss is. But you know what, Irina?"

"They're flakes?"

"All of them. Nobody knows who the new man is. Get it? Your source was probably only extorting your paper for cash."

"We didn't offer him anything, Lieutenant."

The homicide detective frowned but said nothing more.

"Anything you can tell me—"

"I haven't seen the body yet. And you know the drill, Irina. We'll see. Stay back while we look around."

"I'll stay right here."

Irina watched Stojanovic turn and walk to the mobile unit and the activity inside. He walked at a slow pace. He saw no need to hurry, and Irina didn't blame him. Luka's body wasn't going anywhere.

———————

LIEUTENANT VOJIN STOJANOVIC stepped into the mobile home with a greater sense of dread than usual.

He didn't like murder scenes any more than the next cop, but a drug-related murder was worse than most. The cartel would call upon him to sweep a few things under the rug, and he was obliged to do their bidding—they were paying for such service, after all.

The crime scene crew consisted of two men in dark jumpsuits who took pictures of the body and noted the position of where it fell on the floor.

He spoke with the two officers who responded to Irina's call, making notes on how they found the body and whether they thought anything had been disturbed prior to their arrival. Other than the door being open a little, they didn't see anything out of the ordinary, which Stojanovic thought was funny. A dead body on the floor of the living room was perfectly ordinary, sure. The coroner determined the victim died from a gunshot wound to the back of the head, and the killer tied the victim's hands and ankles before the shooting. The bullet remained in the man's skull, the coroner said, and the victim's face was distorted in front by a reddish bulge as a result.

Stojanovic noted the neat and tidy living room, which carried on through the rest of the small house, except for the stack of dirty dishes in the sink. The lieutenant didn't like doing dishes either, so he'd give the victim a pass. There was no sign of forced entry; the victim knew his killer, or didn't suspect his killer was there to kill him when he paid a visit. How much time had passed between the shooting and Irina Vukovic's arrival is what Stojanovic wanted to know, but figured he'd have to wait until the coroner determined time of death. He'd compare it with Irina's statement on her arrival. If it mattered. It probably didn't. But Stojanovic was a thorough detective. He liked to know every detail. Knowing every detail helped him fudge things to keep the cartel clear, or at least alerted to any surprises he couldn't interdict.

If only his wife hadn't gotten sick. If she hadn't gotten sick, he wouldn't have taken their money.

He went back outside to talk to Irina. True to her word, she was still standing where he'd left her.

"Well?" she said as he approached.

"He's dead."

"How?"

"Gunshot. Was the door open when you got here?"

"It squeaked open when I knocked," she said.

"Uh-huh. And you immediately sensed the worst and called the police?"

"I called his name first."

"Luka's name."

"I sure as hell didn't yell for Donald Trump."

"And you got no answer, and you didn't go inside."

"Correct."

"You immediately assumed—"

"Considering the nature of my job, and Luka's employer, yes, Lieutenant, I assumed the worst. If he'd been in the shower we'd only be embarrassed right now."

"He wasn't in the shower. He was fully clothed, on the living room floor, hands and ankles tied."

"No sign of a fight?"

"None."

"He knew the killer."

"You think?" Stojanovic said. "Want to join the force?"

"Give me a break, Lieutenant."

"Go find another source, Irina. This one isn't going to help you. In fact, why don't you forget the whole thing. Nobody needs this kind of trouble, especially a young woman like you."

"I should be at the bar looking for a husband, is that what you think?"

"I used to tell my daughter the same thing. She also used to ignore me."

"Where is she now?"

"Pregnant with her third child. Now get out of here. If I need you again, I'll call you."

Irina pressed her lips together, and he watched her. She didn't volunteer any more, but he already knew she wouldn't. He wanted to know what she was thinking, however. What other moves did she plan to make? She wasn't going to give up the story. This fact bothered him. Because if she didn't, the next body he came to see would be hers. And she did remind him of his daughter.

9

ANOTHER *THUMP* AS IRINA RAN OVER A POTHOLE. MORE COFFEE spilled. "Dammit!" Irina steered to the side of the road with her right hand. The other held her cell phone. She was in the middle of dialing and finished once she brought the little car to a halt. The engine still ran.

Two rings.

"Yes?"

"Rasko, it's Irina. Listen to me. Luka is dead and—"

"What?"

Rasko Lompar was her primary connection to the cartel underworld, introduced to her by a smuggler who was one of Ana Gray's assets.

"They shot Luka at home; you need to get somewhere safe before they find you."

Before Rasko said more, there was a commotion in the background, yelling, and then two pops. *Gunshots.* She knew the sound and there was no mistake. But Irina kept the phone to her head, plugging the other to block out the sound of the engine.

The killer won't pick up and say his name. What are you waiting for?

And then—

"Who is on the line?"

Irina felt a chill. It was a new voice, male; a baritone voice, a man who didn't need to speak loudly for somebody to hear him.

"Is this Irina Vukovic?"

"What have you done?" Irina winced. It was a stupid question, but her racing heart overrode good sense.

"You need to back off, little girl. Otherwise, you'll be seeing me."

The call ended.

Irina let out a breath and almost set the phone in the extra cup holder flooded with the spilled coffee. She jammed the device back into her purse instead.

A target on her back, for sure.

She pulled back onto the road and drove faster than before. Damn the bumps and spills. She had one more person to reach before it was too late.

———————

IRINA BRAKED hard and shoved the gear lever into Park. She ignored the meter and crossed the sidewalk into a large tailor shop with the name KEMAL HASANAJ, TAILORS above the door. The bell chimed as she stepped inside.

Racks of clothes, accessories, all for men, filled the shop; the clerk stood behind a class counter under which more accessories sat on display. The clerk was tall and very thin with a sharp chin. He knew her from the frequent visits she made to talk with Kemal Hasanaj. Before he said a word, Irina blurted, "Tell him we need to talk right now."

"I'm not sure—"

"Go tell him. And tell him Rasko is dead."

A door opened at the rear of the shop. Within moments a lean man in a sharp suit emerged from the racks of men's clothing. He stopped at the counter. Kemal Hasanaj was lean but tough, with sharp features and piercing dark eyes; always impeccably dressed in tailored suits, he was a walking billboard for his shop.

"What did you say, Irina?"

"Rasko is dead." She swallowed.

"Come back to the office."

He turned and started for the back. Irina followed. Hasanaj was only a year or two older than her. Known throughout Podgorica and Montenegro as one of the finest tailors outside of the UK, Hasanaj harbored a secret sure to send him to prison or the grave should he ever make a mistake.

His "real" job was the tailor shop. But he was also a smuggler and black-market information broker. One of Ana Gray's assets, he and Irina had worked together many times whenever Ana required action in the Balkans.

"What went wrong?"

Hasanaj waited for her to take the chair in front of his desk. The office was small but immaculate, with framed photos of the early days of his tailor business on the walls. Irina explained what happened at the mobile home park and the shooting over the phone. Hasanaj listened and his face turned sad.

"Rasko was a friend." He sank into his executive chair.

Irina only nodded. Hasanaj had plugged her in with Rasko Lompar, who put her in touch with Luka. The cartel was following the chain, and she told Hasanaj the trail led back to him.

The smuggler waved off her concern. "They won't dare hurt me. Smugglers have a sort of gentlemen's agreement.

We all know too much about each other for them to risk killing me."

"Yet you have no idea who the new cartel leader may be."

"We don't know everything, Irina."

She remained quiet for a moment. Hasanaj was usually a talker, but news of his friend's murder left him silent and sullen.

Then he said, "Have you updated Ana?"

"She can wait."

"What about the undercover agent?"

"I have no idea what's happening there, either. Ana hasn't called me."

"This started, for me, as just another mission. Now they've killed my friend. I can promise you I'll be taking a bigger role going forward."

Ana's cell phone rang, the ring tone muted by the interior of her purse. She fished out the phone, said, "It's Ana," and answered by clicking the speaker icon. "I'm here with Kemal, Ana," she announced.

"What's the latest on your end?" the Englishwoman asked.

Irina repeated the events of the day for the third time.

Ana said, "Oh, dear."

"I don't know how much the cartel knows about us," Irina said. "I also don't know—"

"If their threat to you has any merit. Yet."

"Want me to lay low for a while?"

"Yes, actually. Because I have an update of my own and it's slightly better news. If nothing else, it will give the cartel somebody else to shoot at. The man I sent into Albania came back with our undercover asset, and I want you to brief them on your end of the case, Irina. I had hoped you might have some new leads, though. Maybe they can go over some of the old ones and shake something loose."

"I may have a new lead for them, actually."

"Tell me more."

"It's fifty-fifty, but I think this man is involved. A former colonel named Peter Kovac. He came up an earlier conversation I had with Rasko. He knows Vercuni and he's worth checking out. Runs a nightclub and I think sells their drugs out of the back room."

"Give everything you have on him to Raven and Elena."

"I know Elena, but who is Raven?"

"The man I sent into Albania. American. Former CIA. He's a good man. Give him all you got. And Irina? For now, leave Kemal out of the conversation."

Hasanaj said, "Why?"

"A good poker player always leaves an ace in reserve."

10

IT WAS A LONG DRIVE TO THE BORDER.

Raven was glad to have left the Triumph motorcycle behind in favor of renting a decent car. He steered the four-door through the twisty mountain roads, letting Elena take in the view and snap pictures, while he focused on the pavement ahead and the view behind. He didn't think anybody was following them. They were the only vehicle on the road, had been for miles and miles; they were clear of any pursuit, but he wasn't for a moment going to say all was well. He wore his pistol under his coat, and the heavy hardware—the Uzi submachine gun—was in the trunk. Just in case.

"May I ask you something?" Elena asked.

"Sure," he said.

"What's your business in all of this? Are you doing it for the money or something else?"

Raven laughed a little. She frowned.

"I'm not making a joke."

"I know you're not," he said. "I work alone. Sometimes Ana hires me."

"What do you mean *alone*?"

"I go looking for trouble."

"Why?"

"Because something happened to me once, and I'm trying to make sure the same thing doesn't happen to others."

"What happened?"

"I'd rather not say, Elena. I don't mean to be rude."

"I understand."

"Ana mentioned your role in this," he said. He wanted to change the subject away from his life. "This mysterious leader. She said it might be somebody you know. From the war."

Now it was her turn to dodge the answers. "Yes."

"What makes you think—"

"It's a rumor same as the CIA people helping him. We're looking for a man who calls himself The Wolf. He was a marauder during the war. He didn't care who he killed or what side they were on. He was only interested in causing as much death and destruction as he could, and he had a large enough crew with him to accomplish the task. He killed my family. For years the story was he died in a battle, but now the rumor is he took over the cartel. My job was to find out if those rumors are true. But I didn't learn anything. They caught me."

"What did they catch you searching through?" Raven asked.

"Computer files. I was desperate for anything. It was a stupid move, and I should have stayed patient."

"I get it."

"Do you?"

"More than you know," he said.

Raven steered through more twisty turns and let the conversation fade. He and Elena had a lot in common and shared a haunted past. He wasn't sure the fact was a matter to celebrate, however.

"Do you have anything left from your family?" he asked.

"Only my DNA," she answered.

She's got more than me, Raven thought.

He felt fortunate to have the sterling silver locket around his neck, concealed by his shirt, which contained the only physical traces of his connection to what he lost. He didn't tell her about the locket, though. He never spoke about it or what was inside, but it served as his conscience. The conduit through which the ghosts of battles past spoke to him and urged him on in the war without end. Only when the ghosts finally fell silent would the war be over. He wondered if they would ever cease their communication. But he was afraid of them going away, too. He wanted the war to stop someday; the killing couldn't go on forever. If they stopped talking, his last link would vanish. He almost wanted the fight to continue until he stopped a bullet rather than give up the last link of communication. Only time would tell. Until then, he had a war to fight. He found allies where available. And he did not give up no matter the challenge. If The Wolf had indeed ascended to the big chair in the Balkan Cartel, Raven wanted to knock him off the throne and into the grave.

ANTON VERCUNI ADMIRED the razor edge of his custom fighting knife. The blade curved at the top to a sharp point; the wooden handle had finger grooves molded from his own hand. He stood in front of a glass display case full of similar custom blades while a conversation took place behind him. Very soon his wife Melika would stop talking and ask him if he was still listening.

"Anton."

Here we go...

"Put the knife away."

He grinned. Well, she sort of said what he expected.

Anton faced the pair seated on the couch. He still held the curved knife.

"I wanted to use *this* on her when we had the chance," he said. "We had her *here*, in the basement. But no. We had to send her to the stupid compound."

Anton stood lean and wiry in casual clothes—sweater over a shirt, creased slacks—with sharp facial features as honed as the blade in his hand. A thin scar on his jaw hinted at either a past knife fight or a clumsy accident with same. He never confirmed one or the other and only his wife knew the truth.

"We follow orders," Melika said. She looked striking even sitting on the couch with crossed legs. Dressed casually same as Anton, the Vercunis clashed with the attire of the third man in the room.

"And what did those orders achieve? The compound is ashes. Our people are dead. The woman is somewhere telling whoever sent her whatever she learned—"

"She learned nothing."

"How do you know?"

"Because you can only speculate using non-specific filler words. She learned nothing, but it's not the point. She's free, and whoever sent her will try again."

Anton slashed at the air, swinging the knife up, down, to the side. He stood far enough away to not strike his wife or their guest. His face twisted with aggression with each slash.

"Will you settle down, Anton?"

He laughed and slashed more before tossing the knife upward. The blade spun end over end before it started to fall, and he snatched it out of the air before it reached the ground.

Anton grew up on the streets of Tirana, Albania, where the poor state of his family forced them to live in the rougher neighborhoods. His brother wound up in a gang and later recruited him, and Anton watched his older brother fall to police gunfire during a drug raid. He later aligned with the Balkan Cartel in pursuit of power and wealth, first as a low-level enforcer. Now he and his wife oversaw "various operations as directed" while sitting on the cartel's leadership council.

Anton returned the curved blade to the display case and asked their guest if he wanted a refill. The dark-skinned man in the blue suit handed Anton a half-empty glass. Anton topped it off at the bar in the corner, then poured his own glass. When Anton took a seat on the second couch opposite his wife and the other man, Melika finally looked satisfied. She continued the conversation.

"We need to know now," she said, "if Irina Vukovic is connected, or a coincidence."

"Irina Vukovic is how that commando knew where to go!" Anton said.

"Then with her two sources dead, they'll pull back and leave us alone for a while."

Their guest finally spoke.

"Don't bet on it."

Anton looked over the top of his glass at Dede Bizi. The Montenegrin couldn't conceal his broad chest and shoulders under his blue silk shirt and tie. The long-sleeved shirt failed to conceal the tattoos running the length of his left arm. His hand and part of his wrist was inked, too. He was a killer and a henchman, never far from Anton or Melika, always ready with a gun or any other convenient murder device he might find.

Melika said, "You think Vukovic will keep digging?"

Bizi nodded.

"Then here's an idea," Anton chimed in. "Undercover spies and commandos don't normally hang out with news reporters. Kill her. Then we get Stojanovic to dig into her background until he learns who put her on our scent. Then we kill *them* too."

Melika asked Bizi, "Why threaten her if you know she won't listen?"

Bizi shrugged. "What if I'm wrong? But I don't think so. If you look at her history, she's never backed down despite threats."

"Wait," Anton said.

Melika and Bizi turned to him. Melika seemed annoyed. He knew why, it was an old argument, and he knew her lines by heart. He was too scatterbrained, unfocused, and needed to propose two or three bad ideas before he landed on a good one. Anton refuted with at least landing on a good idea eventually and she needed to be patient while his thought process worked.

"Not right away," Anton continued. "Don't shoot her right away. See who else she talks to. We can find out a lot more by tracking who she meets with in the next few days."

"We'll end up chasing people not related to any of this," Melika said. "If she talks to somebody at the grocery store, do we follow that person, Anton?"

"Baby, don't insult Bizi's intelligence. He knows the difference." To Bizi, he said, "Right?"

Bizi grinned.

Melika sighed and turned to Bizi. "What do you think?"

"I'll need to hire help if we're tracking multiple people."

"Bring on whoever you need," she told him.

Bizi finished his drink in one final toss back. He set his glass on the coffee table. "Anything more?"

The Vercunis shook their heads.

"I will get started." He rose from the couch and left the room.

Anton and his wife stayed seated. She looked at him. He

stared past her. When he finally said, "When should we alert the others?" she stood up too.

"I'll call them now."

"Good. I'll call Stojanovic," he said. But he didn't leave the couch.

She left him alone with his booze and knives.

11

DEDE BIZI STEERED HIS GRAY MERCEDES DOWN THE CURVING driveway of the Vercuni home. When he reached the automatic gate at the end of the drive, he waited a moment; once the gate swung open, he drove out onto the main road and turned left. Anton Vercuni had a reason to be upset at what happened at the Albanian compound, but not as big a reason as Bizi did. The big enforcer had lost friends, among them David Jocic, the compound's commanding officer. Bizi pulled several rotations at the compound; he knew every inch of the surrounding forest. If he'd been there...

But he hadn't, and his friends died.

Now he had a chance to get even.

Bizi thought about who he wanted to hire as he drove back to the Podgorica city limits. Two names sprang to mind while he discarded other options. He'd have to wait till after dark to locate them, and he'd be going places where the suit he wore would mark him as an easy target. He'd be far out of place in the outfit. Of course, Bizi was anything but easy, and nobody's target.

He could pull off the quiet businessman look until somebody noticed his nose. Broken in several fights, sometimes it got fixed properly, other times not so much. His knuckles bore scar tissue as well; on his right arm, one of the tattoos showed a wolf. It was a symbol of his past involvement in illegal pit fighting where opponents broke his nose more than once. He'd also earned a ton of cash and made connections such as Anton and Melika Vercuni. He was glad to be out of the pits, but he was never far from a fight.

His battles weren't often motivated by revenge, however. He'd have to take extra care. No mistakes.

He wanted to find Elena Corvaci and her commando friend and crush their heads between his hands.

BIZI's first choice was a Serbian freelancer named Rok Pavlovic.

Pavlovic liked to gamble and was always short of money. He'd be an eager recruit, and a good soldier. Bizi had used him before with no complaints.

Bizi wore street clothes as he moved along the busy sidewalk. The dive bars in Podgorica were clustered across a two-block area at the edge of downtown. Tourists didn't bother visiting this area. The clientele was locals, some— well, most—in the process of getting up to no good, but in no hurry to get into trouble. Trouble brought cops. Bizi's jeans were loose enough to allow him to kick. His black T-shirt was tight enough to show off how massive his arms and chest were, and his sleeve tattoos including the wolf on his right arm. An easy target? Hardly.

The flashing yellow neon sign above the door of his destination made him slow his steps. It was easy to get lost in the sidewalk crowd, but Bizi wanted to see the spying eyes from the alley shadows; the creepy lookouts hiding in alcoves.

Word of his approach would hit the club before he pushed in the door. He didn't mind as long as he saw them first, and he had an answer ready for when the doorman challenged his arrival.

He stepped in front of the big doorman with a smile. He felt like a rock in the middle of a stream. The other chattering sidewalk traffic walked around him.

"Mr. Bizi," the doorman said. He was short and thick with muscles, but not as thick as Bizi. "Are you in search of a quiet drink and undisturbed contemplation?"

"Somebody's been reading a dictionary."

The doorman frowned. "If you're here to cause trouble—"

"I'm looking for Pavlovic. He's usually here."

"You got a problem with Pavlovic?"

"Why do you care?"

"Do you?"

Bizi shook his head. "I need him for a job."

"Look, we're fifteen days since the last fight," the doorman said. "We're trying to get to thirty. We want the place to stay nice."

"Do you all get ice cream if you go thirty days?"

"Go choke on your beer."

Bizi smiled again and moved past the doorman. He pushed open the thick wooden door and entered the noisy club.

THE TABLES WERE PACKED but Bizi spotted an open stool at the bar.

A waitress carrying a tray walked in front of him, smacking gum, and told him to find a seat anywhere—if he could. Bizi ignored her. He sat at the bar, wedging between chatting customers on either side, men and women, the ones on his left giving him a dirty look, and Bizi's return glare forcing them away from the bar and somewhere she. Now he had some extra space. The bartender came over.

"You took long enough to get here," the blond man said. His blond hair had green streaks, and he wore a stud in his left nostril. "What kept you?"

"Nothing wrong with taking it slow, pal."

"Uh-huh."

"I'm looking for Pavlovic," Bizi said. "And a beer."

"The beer I got."

The bartender grabbed a mug and filled the glass from a tap behind him. He turned back and set the beer in front of Bizi. "As for Pavlovic, I think he's in the far corner with his back to the wall."

"He in trouble?"

"No, he's just laying low. You know how he is."

"He only lays low—dammit."

"What?"

"I'll try to get him out of here before we break the fifteen-day cycle."

The bartender scoffed. "Oh, that."

"Yeah." Bizi drank down his beer, set the empty glass on the bar, and slid off the stool. If Pavlovic was sitting alone with his back protected, somebody was after him, and the only reason somebody would be after him was because he owed them money.

Bizi shook his head as he started weaving through the crowd.

He and the bartender had to shout at each other to hear themselves over the loud music thumping from ceiling speakers. Bizi didn't understand why it had to be so loud. He didn't want silence, but loudness "just because" wasn't right, either. If he ever opened a bar, it would be a classy place. And he'd keep out of sight, unlike the club owner who watched him now. The gray-haired thin man in a black suit watched Bizi cross the bar from the upper walkway. He leaned against a wooden rail and looked down. Bizi ignored him. Word had reached the owner, all right. They knew he was coming. And the owner wasn't the only one keeping an eye on Bizi. They knew him and his line of work. The bouncers were watching, too. Bizi knew some of them. If they asked him to leave, he wouldn't fight. He might need to hire them later.

He zeroed in on Pavlovic at his back corner table, and the Serbian freelancer looked up as Bizi's shadow fell across him.

"You don't look good, Rok."

Rok Pavlovic showed Bizi what was in his left hand, which he kept concealed under the table. A pistol.

"Bizi, if you're here to collect, I'll leave you bleeding on the floor."

Dede Bizi frowned.

"This was no way to start a conversation," he said.

12

BIZI LEANED ACROSS THE TABLE INTO PAVLOVIC'S FACE.

"Put it away, dumbass."

Pavlovic jammed the pistol behind his back and covered it with his untucked shirt.

"I guess you owe somebody?"

Pavlovic waved it off and drank some more beer. He had two empty mugs discarded to his right.

"Yeah, I owe somebody," he said.

"Who?"

"Why does it matter?"

"I need you for a job. I'll pay off the debt and deduct it from your pay."

"Really?"

"Who do you owe?"

"He's right behind you."

"You keep your pistol hidden, Rok."

Bizi rose and turned. He stood like a wall between Pavlovic and the two men who stopped short in front of him. It was hard to talk over the loud music, so Bizi spoke loudly.

"Ah, my old friend Arso."

"Whoa. I don't have any problems with you, Dede."

"You sure?" Bizi folded his arms. Doing so made his right bicep bulge; the one with the wolf tattoo.

Arso was the operator of a small back-room casino in the city. He lost a little color in his face after Bizi spoke. A second man stayed behind him and to the left. He was in no position to engage Bizi from where he stood. In other words, Arso's backup was useless. He was also shorter than both Arso and Bizi, and nowhere near as bulky. Bizi figured he was a martial artist rather than a knuckle-busting street fighter. As big as he was, Bizi knew he wasn't invincible; then again, neither was the martial artist. The human body had exploitable vulnerabilities no amount of fighting skill could protect.

"All right, give me the terms," Arso said.

"Rok is working for me. I'll pay whatever he owes, and you'll leave him alone."

"He owes me ten grand."

"Ten—" Bizi turned to Pavlovic with a raised eyebrow. "In one night?"

"Five nights, Dede."

"I hope you can afford to eat, because you're not getting any more cash out of me for this job."

"But—"

"Want to deal with him on your own?"

Bizi faced Arso again. He pressed his lips together and held Arso's look. Arso shrugged. They were both frustrated, and Bizi was tempted to side with Arso. If Pavlovic was able to lose such a large amount of money, maybe Bizi needed somebody else, one of the names he rejected earlier. But instead, he sighed and dismissed the thought. Pavlovic was the one for the kill job. Anybody can have a bad night, right?

"We're not going to have any fights here," Bizi said,

"because the club has gone fifteen days without trouble, and I don't want to be the reason they go back to zero, get me?"

"I'd like to go home without any cuts and bruises either, Bizi."

"Good. Here's the deal. I'll get you the ten grand in seventy-two hours."

"I need it tonight."

"I don't have it tonight."

"What assurance do I have you'll pay me in three days?"

Bizi blinked. "Are you insulting me now? You know who I am, right?"

"It's business, Dede, come on."

"I can't hear you over this music."

"All right, all right, three days. I trust you."

"Good. I'll be in touch. And Arso?"

"What?"

"No hassle in the meantime, get me?"

"You got a job, sure. I won't interfere."

Pavlovic jumped out of the booth and pushed his gun into Arso's face. "If you try—"

"Whoa, hey, put it away!" Bizi shouted, shoving Pavlovic back into the booth, darting his eyes around the club to make sure nobody saw them. Especially the owner, who, for all Bizi knew, was still watching from the upper walkway. Bizi couldn't see for sure from where he stood.

"See who you're helping?" Arso said. "A little hothead who can't control himself. How about you keep the ten grand and beat the shit out of him for me?"

"I don't get out of bed for ten grand," Bizi snapped back. He glanced at Pavlovic with a disappointed look. "But you may be right."

"Dede, come on, I'm sorry."

"Three days, Bizi," Arso said.

Bizi stared into Pavlovic's pleading eyes. He knew him as

a cold, calculating killer, a shooter who planned well and didn't hesitate. Now? He was acting like a defanged, cornered tiger.

"I'll see you in seventy-two hours," Bizi told Arso without looking at him.

Arso and his backup cut through the crowd once again. Bizi watched them go, then slid into the booth to face a sheepish Pavlovic.

"The hell are you thinking?"

Pavlovic didn't make eye contact. "They've been on my ass for two weeks, Dede. I've been trying to grow eyes in the back of my head."

"You were going to waste him in front of all these people?"

"Sorry."

"Sorry doesn't cut it, my friend. We got experienced fighters to kill. I need your head straight."

"I'll be fine. I promise." He finally looked up. "I made a bad play and I'm paying in more ways than one."

"Give me the piece. Pass it under the table. Do it now."

Bizi stuck his left hand under the table and waited to feel the cold steel of the handgun. He removed the magazine and the cartridge in the chamber and handed back the gun. His T-shirt didn't allow for the concealment of a nine-millimeter pistol. Pavlovic stuck it behind his shirt again.

"You won't need it tonight," Bizi told him. "And you can keep it in the car, too. Come on. We gotta go find Milos next."

"Why him?"

"Same reason I need you. You're both the best at—you know."

Bizi slid out of the booth and waited for Pavlovic to step in front of him. The pair made their exit with Bizi still looking over his shoulder. He caught sight of the club owner at the upper walkway still. They locked eyes. Bizi waved. The owner didn't acknowledge or smile. His stoic face remained locked on Dede Bizi until his hulking frame passed through the doorway to the street.

————————

THE RED-LIGHT DISTRICT might as well have greeted Dede Bizi and Rok Pavlovic with a parade. Word went out about the gray Mercedes fast. The hustlers would trip over themselves to get first crack at providing a product or service to the men in the car. And there was no doubt it was men in the car.

Bizi parked curbside and when he opened the door, the sounds of heels clicking on pavement reached him before anything else. A foursome of women, each talking over the other. He waved them off and told them to scoot. He and Pavlovic started walking—not far, thankfully—and a man in a trench coat hiding in the doorway offered them drugs. Bizi glared at the man. The man recognized him and apologized. Bizi and Pavlovic continued walking.

They stopped at an all-night pawn shop. Vertical iron bars, like a prison cell, covered the windows and the door. The pawn shop didn't interest them. The apartment above was there they were going, and they turned into the alley beside the shop and hurried up a flight of wooden stairs. The stairs reeked of various smells—urine, cheap perfume, mixed with rotting food scraps in the alley—and Bizi shook his head. Why Milos Gajda kept visiting the apartment above the pawn shop, he didn't understand.

Anja Kankaras, who lived there, wasn't a very good hooker.

The door at the top of the stairs was solid, the hinges and knob of recent vintage, locked, padlocked, and chained. No light or sound inside, but it didn't mean the place was empty. Pavlovic stayed at the midway point on the stairwell to watch Bizi's back and his own. Bizi knocked on the door, hard, making as much noise as he could without kicking the damn thing off its hinges. There was no excuse to destroy private property without a valid reason.

Then Bizi heard a man scream.

Pavlovic heard it too and rushed up the steps and Bizi decided to find out if he could bust through the door after all. A step back, a raised foot—

It took three hard kicks, the last two sending jolts of pain up Bizi's leg, but the doorframe splintered, and the door swung open. But Bizi hesitated despite his first step forward. The apartment was dark. But the man screamed a second time and managed to yell, "Help me!"

Light glowed from a hallway...

Bizi ran ahead, Pavlovic behind him, Pavlovic shouting, "Give me my ammo!" but Bizi ignored him. The glow in the hall came from a room at the end and Bizi ran there and stopped so quick in the doorway Pavlovic bumped into him and almost fell on his ass.

Bizi stared at the sight before him.

"Don't just stand there!" yelled Milos Gajda.

"If you take one step," yelled the naked woman straddling Milos, "I'll cut his throat!"

She held a large knife.

"Help me, Dede! She's crazy!"

Dede Bizi's shoulders sank. How in the hell had he ever thought these two clowns were good for the job...

"Anja!" Bizi shouted. He didn't step into the room. "Put the knife down. This isn't how we want to do this!"

"He's trying to cheat me!"

"She's trying to rip me off!"

"You bastard!" She plunged the knife down.

Milos Gajda screamed like a frightened child as he clamped both hands on Anja's slender right wrist and pushed back to keep the tip of the knife from his neck. He was strong, but so was she, despite her scrawny build.

"Anja!"

And with her attention on Milos, Bizi, and Pavlovic ran into the room. Bizi tackled Anja off the bed, blocking the knife as she swung it his way. They hit the carpet on the other side of the bed and Bizi rolled off her. The carpet smelled of old dust and tickled Bizi's nose. She came at him screaming, seemingly unaware of being stark naked, but there was nothing alluring about her tiny frame. The girl needed to eat something, but preferred heroin. Track marks dotted her body. Bizi grabbed her knife arm and twisted, forcing her to the side; he pushed her to the floor, on her face, knife arm behind her back. He yanked the knife free and then smacked her. Anja stopped making noise and went limp and started sucking in whatever was embedded in the carpet. When she started coughing, he rolled her onto her side. She cursed his family in a mumbling string of obscenities. He propped her up against the bed.

"Somebody throw me a blanket," Bizi said.

Rok and Milos tossed him the bed's comforter, but it was as smelly as the carpet. Bizi sneezed and covered the nude woman. He set the knife in a corner behind a stack of junk.

"You want to get dressed?" he said to Milos.

"What?" Milos noticed his own naked body and said, "Oh, right," and rolled off the bed. He collected his clothes from the floor and started pulling them back on.

"Have you two gone bughouse or something?" Bizi asked.

"What's the problem?" Milos had his boxers backward. He hurried to correct the error, and seeing the hairy man's privates again wasn't a sight Bizi had ever hoped to see again.

Bizi shook his head. He wanted to walk away, but there

wasn't time to go find another crew. Rok and Milos had performed well in the past, but Bizi had to admit he had no idea how they lived when he wasn't employing them. Now he knew.

"Let's get out of here," he told them. He gestured at the still-mumbling Anja. "Can't you afford better?"

"Couldn't afford her!" Milos said with a laugh, and Pavlovic laughed too. But Bizi wasn't laughing, and neither was Anja and the big man with the sleeve tattoos wanted to get away from her before she figured out where the knife was.

"She got a crusty snatch anyway," Milos said as they left the room.

13

Vojin Stojanovic dropped into his creaky desk chair and slumped. He hadn't bothered to remove his overcoat. He stared at his semi-cluttered desk in a daze.

"You all right?"

He raised his head. His chief, Captain Rostoder, in his usual black suit with hair slicked back, his dark eyes examining Stojanovic critically, stood over his right shoulder.

"Tough morning," the homicide lieutenant said.

"Did you make the arrest?"

"He's in booking now."

"Good. One more down. Now you can get back to the drug killings. The ones you've barely moved on since they happened."

Stojanovic rotated his chair to see the captain better. He didn't stand.

"I've talked to my informants, they're doing what they can," Stokanovic said. "They're *cartel* killings. We don't solve them overnight."

"Stop it, Vojin. They're homicides like any other, yet whenever you draw one—"

"What?"

"Very little happens."

Now Stojanovic stood. A red flush crawled up his neck. He wasn't as tall as Captain Rostoder, and already he saw the others in the room watching them.

"Meaning what, Captain?"

"Meaning when I look at your unsolved log, I see a pattern. Want me to reassign those homicides? We can let one of the younger teams take a crack. What do you think?"

"I think you need to back off and let me do my job."

"Some of us are very curious what you think your job actually may be, Lieutenant."

The captain turned and walked away, weaving around the other desks, those others who so eagerly watched seconds ago quickly finding other matters for their attention. Nobody looked at Stojanovic, and he didn't look at anybody else. He was watching Rostoder's back.

Stojanovic removed his overcoat and hung it on a hook on the wall behind him. He set his sport jacket over the back of his chair and sat. The chair creaked again, and anger flashed across his face.

His phone rang. He grunted again. The cell was in the pocket of his overcoat. He rose to retrieve it and dropped into the chair once more. He didn't have to glance at the caller ID. He knew who was on the other end.

"Yes?"

"You sound grumpy," said Anton Vercuni.

"I *am* grumpy."

"Nice arrest this morning. How long did it take to nail this one?"

"Forget it. What do you want?"

"You're hard to reach. I tried yesterday and last night. Are you ignoring me, Lieutenant?"

"I've been busy."

"You sound stressed."

"I'm also tired."

Vercuni laughed and Stojanovic squeezed the phone. He kept his voice low and his head down. For all anybody knew, he was talking to his wife. The calls from her were regular enough, and he never excused himself to take them; private calls at his desk were part of his pattern, and he didn't want to change his behavior now as it appeared the upper brass had an eye on him.

Great. More stress.

"I need you to be ready for a big one," Vercuni said. "You'll know when it happens, and I'll tell you more when the time comes."

Stojanovic closed his eyes. He was being advised of a murder taking place, soon, and there was nothing he could do about it less he exposed himself for being on the cartel's take.

This was a first. It was one thing to try and sweep the cartel's hits under the rug when he knew the dead were bad guys who probably deserved what happened, but this time had had no idea who the victim might be.

"Why are you telling me this? You know better than to tell me this."

"Keep your voice down, Lieutenant."

"Why are you telling me this? You've never done this. At least tell me it's not—" Stojanovic stopped.

"Not what?"

"You know what I mean."

"If you aren't careful, they'll figure out I'm not your wife."

"Tell me." Stojanovic took a deep breath and mentally bit his tongue. *Steady. Steady, man.*

"I just told you. Be ready. I'll call you again."

Vercuni hung up. Stojanovic tossed the phone onto a stack of folders and left his desk. He needed fresh air, a cup of coffee, and wished he hadn't quit smoking. He wondered if he could bum a cigarette from one of the others. His wife would scream, but at least getting yelled at for smoking would cover up what she should *really* be yelling at him for.

He filled a chipped white mug with coffee and went out to the center courtyard, the concrete square surrounded by sections of the headquarters building on four sides. He stood in the sun, against a wall, and the heat felt good. The coffee was too hot, so he blew on the liquid.

He didn't know what Vercuni was talking about, but he knew it wouldn't be a good thing. But he'd made his deal a long time ago. He had no choice but to do what they told him.

And Captain Rostoder?

Did the department think he was dirty?

And how long had they known? Had he failed to cover his tracks from the beginning, or had he screwed up in the recent past?

He'd have to wait and find out, unless he discovered a way to escape before his own department slapped handcuffs on him.

NOBODY ELSE HAD CALLED to threaten her, but Irina Vukovic wasn't taking any risks. She hadn't gone home after the murders and her visit with Kemal Hasanaj; instead, she'd checked in to a hotel and asked a friend at the newspaper to collect clothes and other items from her apartment. She planned to stay at the hotel a few days, at least.

She wished she had another car, though. The compact might be known to the cartel. She knew a few tricks to see if anybody followed her, and she left the hotel an hour before her lunch date with Ana Gray's other two operatives. Elena, the undercover agent, and the man who plucked her out of the cartel's compound, Sam Raven. She left early so as to have enough time to run her counter-surveillance maneuvers.

Irina attempted to learn more about Sam Raven, but there was nothing publicly available about the man. Without going through official channels or asking for a favor from certain people, she'd turned up zero. He was a mystery, so far. She'd get her answers soon enough. And maybe, she decided, a little mystery was okay. There was probably enough about him she didn't want to know; she knew Ana trusted him, and decided it was enough.

She drove in circles around several blocks along the way, quickly getting bored with the task, but she kept up the routine until she was sure. Even then, she kept checking her rearview mirror and performing the odd circle around the block. Cartel killers knew tricks of their own. They could be following her in multiple cars, for example, trading off. She wasn't simply looking for one car hanging about, she was looking for multiples, naming makes and models and descriptions out loud to better remember them. When none of the vehicles repeated after the extra hour passed, she started to settle down.

When she reached the restaurant, she was hungry indeed. And shaking. She felt like a walking mass of frayed nerves.

They saw her before she saw them.

RAVEN RECOGNIZED Irina Vukovic from pictures provided by Ana. When the reporter entered the restaurant, he noticed right away the harried look on her face, the out-of-place strands of hair. She scanned the restaurant with darting eyes. Raven raised one of his hands. It wasn't the most clandestine form of contact, but it appeared very normal to anybody watching. And if the cartel had operatives looking at them, he didn't mind. He wanted a crack at a few more of them, up close this time. Both he and Elena were armed and ready for a fight.

Raven had two rules he lived by, one of which was No Gunfights in Public. If the enemy wanted to challenge them now, he'd have to put a stop to it, fast. He didn't want innocent casualties in the crossfire. He was out to avenge victims, not create more. When it was possible, he preferred to lead the enemy into lesser-populated areas, battlefields of his own choice. Then there was plenty of room to groove.

"She looks rough," Elena said.

Raven only grunted in reply. Irina crossed the restaurant to their table, shifting her body here and there to avoid crashing into the backs of occupied chairs. The tables were set close together, and the passing space between them was at a premium. While Raven and Elena sat together with their backs to the wall, Irina was exposed to the front door. She made no comment as she slid into the chair and set her purse on the empty chair to her left.

"I'm Irina," she said, breathing hard. None of them shook hands. They were supposed to be old friends.

"Did you run here?" Elena said.

"No, had to make sure I wasn't followed." Irina produced a compact and small comb from her purse and tidied her hair. By the time she put the items away, the waitress arrived with their menus and took their drink orders.

The restaurant was crowded and buzzing with conversation. Tiled floor of checkered black and white, with white walls and black wainscotting; it wasn't much for decor, but it was a popular place. The kitchen was equally loud, and visible through a half wall, though the partial wall wasn't low enough to see all the activity or any faces. Chefs' hats moved back and forth; steam drifted into the light fixtures. Cooking tools clanged against cooktops. Raven was happy for the noise. It covered the conversation he needed to have with the reporter.

"Did anybody follow you?" Raven asked.

"No. You can't believe how long I drove in circles checking."

Raven grinned. He could believe it for sure. "What's the latest?" he asked. "Anything new on your end?"

"Are you kidding? What did Ana tell you?"

Raven provided details from his and Elena's end of the mission so far, which wasn't much. Then Irina took over and explained her efforts to find the name of the new cartel boss, and the deaths of her contacts. Per Ana's request, she left out Kemal Hasanaj's name, despite her instincts to the contrary. Raven and Elena gave her a sense of trust and security. Irina had only felt such a "vibe" when in the presence of "good guys"—and she knew enough "bad guys" to feel the difference. Her gut, head, and heart agreed. She could trust them. She didn't understand why Ana wanted her to keep Kemal's name secret but assumed the British socialite and spymaster had her reasons.

When Irina finished, Raven said, "Are we back at square one?"

"Not at all," Irina said. Before she continued, the waitress returned with their drinks, and they ordered lunch. Irina only asked for a soft drink, but Raven thought she needed an elixir much more powerful. The girl needed a bottle of wine just to start.

"I have one potential lead," the reporter said. "It's a name we picked up early in my investigation, but my sources were 50/50 on whether he was worth checking out, so I set him aside."

"Who is it?" Elena asked.

"A man named Peter Kovac. Former colonel in the military. Now he runs a nightclub and is most likely a distributor for the cartel's product."

"But you said this was fifty-fifty," Raven said. "Why?"

"None of my sources were a hundred percent sure about him."

Raven nodded. Fair enough. If Kovac was part of the cartel and good at keeping his head down, he was probably a much better link in the chain than Irina realized. She wasn't thinking the same way Raven thought about such things. The least likely candidates were often the exact cages he needed to rattle.

Whoever Kovac was, he'd rattle the man hard.

"I hope the food here is good," Irina said, glancing around at the crowded tables. "Seems like it."

"I'm sure it's fine," Raven said, and steered the conversation back to Kovac. He wanted to know where the man worked, lived, anything about his habits.

Irina only knew where he worked. She named the nightclub and gave them the address. Elena noted it in her phone. The rest Raven and Elena would have to discover themselves.

14

IRINA'S ATTENTION SHIFTED TO ELENA. "WHAT HAPPENED WITH you?"

"You mean how did I get caught?"

It was an awkward part of the conversation for the waitress to return, but the two women shifted in their seats to cover the pause and look at the menus once again. Raven already knew what he wanted. He let the women order first. After the waitress departed once again, Elena returned to the question. She gave Irina the same explanation she offered Raven. "I screwed up." Which was enough to satisfy the reporter. When she expressed frustration with her own lack of progress, Raven jumped in.

"Just the way it goes."

Irina laughed without humor. "Easy for you to say. You're not the one with a target on your back."

"Are you sure?"

The reporter paused a moment, then shrugged.

"How are you fixed in terms of protection?" Raven asked her.

"What protection? This isn't the first time somebody has threatened me. Nobody is going to kill a reporter."

"Famous last words?"

"They only want me to back off," Irina said. "If I get reassigned to cover the installation of a new street light or something benign, they'll leave me alone. I've been through this before."

Raven was going to say more, but three men entering the restaurant caught his attention. The trio tried to act normal, but one of them glanced at their table and took too long to look away. Another had sleeve tattoos displayed—not uncommon, but enough for Raven to take notice. From where she was sitting, Irina couldn't see them. Elena saw Raven looking and grabbed his arm.

"What is it?" Irina asked. Then she turned.

"Who are they?" Raven directed the question to Elena.

"The one with the tattoos. Dede Bizi. He's Anton Vercuni's hatchet man."

Irina added: "They must have followed me after all."

"All right," Raven said, as he watched the hostess take the trio to a table out of sight. "Let's enjoy our lunch. They won't try anything here."

"Famous last words?" Irina said.

"I hope not," Raven told her.

DEDE BIZI, earlier in the day, told Melilka Vercuni he needed three more men.

"You already hired two," she said, "why do you need more?"

"We need to follow the reporter so I need a rotating team. I'll only need them today."

"I don't want to pull from my security team. Where else

do you expect me to get three men for you at such short notice?"

"It's only a few hours, Melika."

"Fine!" she said. "Take whoever you want."

Bizi asked for good drivers. Two of the house guards had the experience he wanted; the third said he watched a lot of American NASCAR so that counted. With Bizi, Miles, and Rok in three cars of their own, plus the three from Melika and Anton's house, they managed to track Irina Vukovic from her hotel to the restaurant. The reporter made it a challenge, however. She knew a few basic counter-surveillance tricks, but nothing the team couldn't overcome. They coordinated via handheld radio to keep her in sight.

Finding her hotel wasn't hard, either. The Vercunis had connections at many hotels in Podgorica. There were always plenty of hotel guests looking for recreational drugs, asking bellhops and others on the sly if they knew where to find any, and the Vercunis supplied those wants via hotel employees who knew who to call. Sending Irina's picture to these connections scored the lead Bizi needed. All it took after locating the hotel was watching for her car to leave the garage.

At the restaurant, Bizi and Miles and Rok went inside and spotted Irina with the other two, and it didn't take a PhD to identify Elena Corvaci. Bizi remembered her. The man beside her had to be the commando who destroyed the Albanian forest compound. All they had to do was wait. Elena and her friends were officially living on borrowed time and about to eat their last meal.

ONLY RAVEN and Elena finished their lunch. Irina ate half and picked at the rest.

He already had a plan for their exit. Go out the back. The goons' arrival meant Irina was compromised and the opposition wasn't going to give up despite her earlier insistence. They wanted to know who she was talking to. Elena knew Dede Bizi from when the Vercunis held her prisoner prior to moving her to the compound. And now Bizi knew *his* face as well.

Good. All the players were on the field; now it was time to run the ball.

Raven handed Elena the keys to their rental and paid the check. The only problem with going out the back was passing the goons' table. There was no sense in being clandestine anymore. Raven wanted to force them into action.

When they passed the table in question, Raven winked at Dede Bizi. The man's frown in return was all Raven needed. Everybody knew what was expected of them now.

The back door opened on a smelly alley. Raven told the women to hurry and get the car. He waited with the Nighthawk .45 in his hand, but didn't click off the safety.

The back door opened a second time, and the action started right away.

RAVEN BROUGHT the .45 down across the first head available. It wasn't Bizi who tumbled to the alley floor, but one of the other two. Bizi and the third man moved fast, stepping around their fallen comrade to launch at Raven, who met them with a kick and another swing of the .45. Bizi ducked, the gun passing over his head; he crashed into Raven's midsection. His momentum pushed Raven back into the wall behind him. Bizi drew back his fist. Raven hit Bizi with the .45 once, twice. The big man wasn't fazed. Raven jerked his head out of the way to avoid Bizi's punch, and Bizi screamed as his already-scarred knuckles smashed into the brick wall. Raven slammed a knee into Bizi's groin and smacked him with the gun a third time, and Bizi's grip slackened. It was enough for Raven to shove him away and face the third man.

Raven ducked the third man's first swing, but not his follow-up kick. The man's shoe clocked him in the jaw. Raven tumbled to the ground and rolled as the third man tried to stomp him. Raven jabbed the snout of the .45 hard into the third man's belly, forcing him back enough to regain his feet and execute a kick of his own, a textbook spinning high kick, sending the third man flying against the wall.

Raven came out of his spin to face Bizi once more, but the big man was slower. He swung twice, his big arms flashing by in an arc; Raven ducking; then Bizi lunched once more to try and grab Raven while he was crouched. Raven sprang upward, catching Bizi's chin with his head. Bizi's teeth clacked together, and Raven used his left elbow to hit the big man in the face. Another swing of the .45 against his hard head and down went Bizi.

The three men were down but not out. Their groans filled the alley. Raven staggered a little as he made his way forward, stepping around them, jamming the .45 back into his shoulder harness. The rental car with Elena behind the wheel screeched to a stop at the mouth of the alley. Irina, in the back seat, held the door open and Raven climbed in beside her. Elena accelerated into traffic as Raven pulled the door shut. Finally, he let out a groan of his own.

"Those guys can hit hard," he said.

Irina checked him for major injuries. "You hurt bad?"

Raven pushed her away. "I'm all right."

"Nothing a shot of whiskey won't cure?"

"Or something similar," he said. He slumped in the seat.

"Where to?" Elena asked.

"Our hotel for now," Raven said. "We gotta figure out

something for Irina. You aren't going anywhere near your home, office, or wherever you were staying."

"I agree," the reporter said.

"Raven?" The alarm in Elena's voice brought Raven out of his slump.

"What?"

"There are three cars trying to catch up to us."

"Good."

"Are you nuts?" Irina said.

"My trigger finger is itching. Might as well give it a workout. Where's a good place for a fight around here?"

Irina blinked at him.

15

RAVEN ASKED IRINA TO SCOOT AWAY FROM THE CENTER OF THE back seat, where he pulled down the armrest and accessed a panel to the trunk. The panel lifted upward, and Irina held it while Raven reached through and hauled back a tote bag. Inside, the Uzi submachine gun and a set of magazines. He held the Uzi below the window while Elena sped up and made a few turns.

"They're staying with us," she said.

Raven watched the three cars weave through traffic to keep them in view. Irina watched too. She was breathing hard and plenty nervous.

"Take it easy," he told her.

"They're onto us because of me!"

"Not helpful right now, Irina."

Elena made another turn. The street widened a little, a mix of homes and apartments on either side, and Raven shook his head. This was not the place for a fight. But as the chase cars made the turn and sped to catch up, he decided he might not have a choice. Elena made another turn, a right, down a short street, then a left, blowing through a stop sign and making other drivers screech to a stop. Shops and strip malls now. Raven told her to take the next left and find a spot behind the strip mall. A loading area, back parking lot— anything. There'd be less people around. With the Uzi, he had a chance to make it a short fight.

Elena powered down a side street, jerked the wheel right, and the car bumped a curb heading into the rear lot of the strip mall. A few cars, packing debris at back doors. *Good enough*, Raven decided.

"Slow down."

Elena did so. Raven pushed open his door, yelled, "Keep going!" and rolled out onto the blacktop. Irina yelled something at his back, but Elena was already speeding away, the back door slamming shut on its own as the car accelerated.

Raven took cover behind a stack of wooden pallets and hoped no store employees came out for a cigarette. The three chase cars turned into the lot, the lead car speeding up to catch Elena. Raven fired the Uzi. He wasn't aiming for the first or middle car, but the third. He wanted to disable it and keep the others from going out the way they came in. The Uzi stuttered in his grip, the 9mm slugs spitting from the muzzle scoring on the third car's front tires. The rubber exploded, louder than the gunshots for a moment, the front end of the car sinking forward. The vehicle stopped. Raven raised his aim and stitched a line of slugs across the wind screen, but the driver was already out and rolling, returning fire with a pistol. Raven dropped low as the shots smacked into the wall. The other two cars screeched to a halt, the driver of the third running to cover behind the middle car.

Raven pivoted as the first car, stopping a little beyond him, became the primary threat. The driver jumped up to fire, and Raven tagged him with a short burst across the chest. Then he ran to the fallen driver, keeping low around the car's front grill. The dead gunner lay still. The other two fired at him while he reloaded, their shots smacking into the body of the car and breaking glass. Raven fired a burst to force them back, then raced around the car's passenger side. One of the other gunners was moving too, coming around the back of the middle car. He and Raven had a second to look each other in the eye before Raven shot him high in the chest and knocked him down. Raven moved around the back of the car. The last gunner got off a shot. Raven felt the bullet pass his head. The Uzi stuttered again in return and the last gunner's body jerked as the slugs ripped into him. He sprawled on the ground near the front tires. Raven ran, leaving the carnage behind, racing to where Elena had stopped the rental. Already the shop doors were popping open, curious heads peeking out. Raven ignored them. He jumped into the back seat beside Irina once more, the still-smoking Uzi tight in his grip, and Elena hit the accelerator. He and Irina, not belted in, lurched backward with the sudden surge of speed.

"I can't believe you did that!" Irina said.

Raven reloaded the Uzi, upped the safety catch, and returned the weapon to the tote bag. He set the bag between him and Irina. There was no joy on his face. He looked grim.

"I can do all kinds of things," he told her.

IRINA FINALLY BUCKLED her seat belt and tried to settle her racing pulse with deep breaths, but it didn't help. She'd have to calm down over time. Nobody, she figured, survives a brush with murder and dismisses the event like a sneeze. Then she had to correct her thought. Raven and Elena behaved as if the gun fight and getaway was a leisurely stroll in the park.

When Elena pulled the car over after getting away from Raven, they turned to watch the fight. Irina was on her knees in the back seat trying to see Raven, when a stray bullet nicked the back window. Elena told her to put her head down unless she wanted another hole she wasn't born with. Irina followed directions and stayed as low as she could while still witnessing the fight. Watching Raven engage the three men who wanted to kill them was both thrilling and frightening. There was no other way for her to describe it. Here was a man just as capable of killing as the three chasing them, yet by some twist of fate, they were enemies instead of allies.

She'd seen plenty of violence, or at least the after-effect, but never became numb to it. As she watched Raven in the seat next to her, it was obvious he wasn't happy. Killing was something he had to do, not something he liked. It made her understand him a little better.

Raven said, "What's on your mind?"

"No—nothing."

"Uh-huh."

"Are you sure our hotel is the best place for her, Raven?" Elena asked.

Irina's first thought was of Kemal Hasanaj. He could hide her. Hide her very well, indeed. But Ana Gray wanted her to keep him secret for now...

And she didn't want to put Kemal at further risk, either. No matter what they decided to do, the cartel wasn't going to stop.

"It'll due for a short time," Raven said. "Long enough for us to figure something out."

"I have spare clothes," Elena told the reporter. "Looks like we're about the same size."

Irina didn't reply.

"Elena," Raven said, "you stay with her tonight, and I'll go visit this Kovac fellow."

Irina said, "Then what?"

"Good question," Raven answered. "It depends on what I find when I see the nightclub up close."

Elena drove on.

16

DEDE BIZI WASN'T WASTING ANY TIME.

Getting away from the restaurant after the fight proved a challenge. A witness called the police, and by the time Bizi, Milos, and Rok were mobile, the cops had arrived. No chance to make a getaway. Bizi did call one of the other three drivers, though, and told them to get after Elena and Irina and the commando and leave them dead in the street. While Bizi and his men explained to the police they were the victims of an unprovoked attack, Bizi hoped the other three gunners were getting the job done.

Of course, he learned later they not only failed, but were no longer alive for Bizi or Anton and his wife to yell at, but Anton and his wife would sure yell at *him* for losing three of their house guards. Did such troopers cost a premium? Bizi didn't care. He had a job to do and wasn't going to settle for defeat. They still had their contacts at the Podgorica hotels; a lot of contacts. Bizi would do what he did last time. Send out Irina Vukovic's picture, advise of a reward if anybody found her, wait for a call. Meantime, Bizi and Milos and Rok needed to lick their wounds and get ready for the next bout.

RAVEN DECIDED it had been smart to book adjoining rooms. He and Elena were next to each other, which meant Irina could stay with her and he was close if anything happened. The trick was to make sure *nothing* happened except to the bad guys.

Raven walked behind the two women as they entered the hotel from the garage. It was one of the smaller hotels in the city, near the M18 motorway, and out of the way. Raven thought it was good to stay away from a high-traffic area where they might be spotted by cartel soldiers. The lobby was quiet and clean and mostly black and white, the motif on the floor and walls continuing with the furniture spread about as well. Raven steered them toward the bank of elevators.

Had Raven looked behind him, he'd have noticed the janitor mopping a corner watching them go to the elevators. He waited for them to step inside, then made a call on his cell phone. He spoke for a short amount of time and put the phone way before his supervisor caught him.

In the elevator, Irina said, "How do I not feel like a prisoner here?"

"There's room service," Elena said.

Irina didn't laugh.

"First time in protective custody?" Raven asked.

"I've heard the phrase a thousand times, but never thought it would apply to me. This is…"

"Insane," Elena finished.

"Insane is a good word."

Raven said, "It will be over before you know it," and the elevator dinged. The doors slid open once more and the trio started down the hallway.

Raven figured he'd leave Elena to watch Irina while he

went prowling for Colonel Kovac. It might also be nice to pay a visit to Anton and Melika Vercuni; maybe give them something in return for how they treated Elena. He could be out all night if he wanted.

Raven let Elena show Irina her room and clothes before gathering them in his room for a short council of war.

Irina showed him where to find Kovac's club, and an internet search turned up an article, with a picture, of Kovac at a NATO ceremony bringing Montenegro into the organization. The picture was a few years old, but Raven decided his basic appearance wouldn't have changed. He probably was not as skinny, depending on whether or not he maintained any of his old military discipline in civilian life.

Elena said, "Are you taking the Uzi or can I keep it?"

"I don't plan on any shooting," Raven said. "This is a walk around and see sort of thing."

Irina blinked, watching both of them, stunned they could talk about weapons and violence was if one was telling the other not to forget milk on the way home from work. She was more surprised now than she'd been after the gunfight at the strip mall; this was a way of life for them.

The reporter realized she'd entered an entirely different world from the one she was used to. Being on the periphery of the cartel's world hadn't prepared her for this. There had always been the safety of the newsroom to return to, the protection of the press pass, the idea she was only an observer recording the facts and not instrumental in any outcome. Getting involved with Ana Gray changed everything, at least in this case. This was much more than passing or collecting information for one of Ana's operatives before going back to her regular life. She had no idea if she *could* go back to normal after this. Raven and Elena and their familiarity with violence had to win the day. Otherwise, Irina had no idea how she'd function with having to look over her shoulder for the rest of her life.

Raven closed the meeting saying he needed a nap before going out, so Elena brought Irina back to her room to try on some clothes. Raven shut the connecting door and hoped the activity helped lift Irina out of her shock. He knew it wasn't easy for her to be exposed to what she'd witnessed in the last few days, and he wanted to bring the mission to a close for her sake as much as Elena's.

He preferred going to the nightclub without Elena anyway, in case his walk-around-and-see approach turned to crap and he had to haul out the .45 once more.

He hoped it didn't happen.

LATER, Elena didn't know how to entertain Irina, or what they should talk about. She didn't know how to "girl talk" or whatever women did when they were together. She sat on the bed against the headboard while Irina fidgeted in a chair and turned on the TV. After a while, Elena wasn't paying attention to the screen. She didn't think Irina was either.

"Can you turn this off?" Irina asked.

"Why?"

"I want to talk to you about something."

Elena used the remote; the TV winked off. "What?"

"Look, I thought I'd seen some stuff, okay? I thought I knew what the worst was. But you and Raven? You act like it's just another day of the week."

Elena frowned. "It is."

Irina left her chair and started to pace. "How, though? If I was Raven, I'd be a wreck, yet he's out looking for more. What gives?"

"It's hard to explain," Elena said, "if you've never been on the edge of death or starvation."

Irina stopped pacing and looked at Elena. "What do you mean?"

"For you, finding out the identity of the new cartel leader is just another expose, right?"

Irina folded her arms. "I guess. Ana only asked for whatever I could find. Just information."

"Well, if it's who she and I suspect, and she obviously didn't tell you this, it might be the man who murdered my family."

"Oh."

"So, yeah. You don't understand."

"Um…can you tell me what happened?"

Elena thought for a moment. She didn't want to, and the knowledge would either help Irina catch up, or further drive her away. She decided to take a chance and see if it helped the reporter settle down.

"We had a farm. This was during the Yugoslav War, Serbia steamrolling through Croatia. A man who called himself The Wolf had a group of mercenaries. They were murderers. It didn't matter who you were; they killed anybody they found. Well, they found our farm. My father and brothers tried to fight them off, but they were killed. My mother got me and my sister out of the house, but they shot my sister and grabbed my mother and I ran to hide at the neighbor's house. They had already fled. We stayed behind. Now I wish we'd run, too, but my father's family had lived on the land for 200 years.

"I saw them shoot my father, brother, and sister; I listened to them rape my mother, and there wasn't anything I could do. I hid and hoped they didn't find me. They looted what they wanted from the house and moved on. Never mind how I spent the rest of the war. So, I'm sorry—I understand why you don't understand, but I can't explain it to you."

"And you think this man runs the cartel now?"

"It's a rumor. We're trying to see if it's true. It's not simply a matter of publicizing his name. It's about exposing a war criminal and making him pay for what he's done, now, and in the past. Get it?"

Irina sat again, but on the edge of the chair this time. She looked lost. Elena wasn't about to explain further. She was stirred up enough. She'd spent years trying to bury the horror; now she was forced to relive it several different ways. She hadn't needed to tell Raven. He understood. He didn't need to know more than the basics, and it was enough. But Irina lived insulated from such events; she was lucky. Elena wished she'd been lucky, but fate or the universe or whatever controlled the movement of the planets had other plans. And she had to live with the aftermath. The horror was tough enough to have witnessed. Surviving the horror was sometimes worse.

"I didn't mean to—"

Elena waved her off. "You needed to know."

"Ana always—"

"Never gives us more than we need, I know. We had a long talk before I took the assignment. She wanted to make sure—"

"Make sure of what?"

"I wasn't going to crack under the strain."

"Have you?"

"It's still early."

Elena grinned at her dark humor but Irina wasn't smiling. Elena rolled off the bed and said she wanted a shower before going to sleep. Irina didn't reply. Elena grabbed the bathrobe provided by Ana and shut the bathroom door. She'd been waiting for a chance to get under the hot spray since they'd arrived. While she waited for the water to warm, she stripped off her clothes and left them in a pile on the tiled floor. The steam quickly covered the mirror and blocked her reflection. She hadn't wanted to look at herself anyway.

When she'd hid in the neighbor's house, a long sprint through tall grass, which left her out of sight from The Wolf and his marauders, she'd found refuge in the basement. It was dark, the floor dirty, and she'd crawled into the darkest corner available. It was dirty there, too, and she remembered bugs moving across her skin, through her hair, yet she didn't dare move or make a sound. She remained in the dark with the bugs for hours. Hours turned into a day, and then she emerged into the unknown. Since then, she always felt the bugs. She couldn't shower enough to clean them off. She hoped, if The Wolf really was alive, killing him would make the bugs go away for good.

IRINA HAD TO MOVE. She had to leave. She couldn't sit still any longer and let the walls close in on her.

With the shower running and Elena occupied for at least twenty minutes, she grabbed the extra key card from the dresser and hurried from the room. Irina guided the door shut behind her so Elena wouldn't hear it close, then headed down the hall. She needed a break. Fresh air. A few minutes would suffice. There was much to think about and consider, and Irina was tired of feeling like an animal in a cage. *Jesus, honey, it's only been a couple of hours...you'd never have survived in the basement.*

But with all the revelations and violence she'd witnessed, the "couple of hours" felt much longer. She was at her breaking point.

A walk around the hotel. Fresh air. That's what she

needed. She stepped into the elevator and headed for the lobby.

It was the janitor, now vacuuming the carpet of the lobby sitting area, who saw Irina leave and sent an alert to Dede Bizi.

Bizi earlier made it clear he and his men couldn't wait in the lobby. Irina knew their faces. When the janitor saw her exit the lobby elevator and head for main exit to the street, he sent a text to Bizi advising him of her departure. Then he busied himself with his tasks. He didn't want to know what would happen next. He told himself to keep his mouth shut and think about the $200 US in his pocket, provided by Bizi, with a grim look giving him more of a warning than any string of words might provide.

17

THE NIGHTCLUB WASN'T WHAT RAVEN EXPECTED.

Irina had told him it was more upscale than some of the other popular clubs in the city; she was right. No street clothes allowed. A jacket and tie were standard for the men, and the women took advantage of the variety of fancy dress options available to them. They wore the latest and greatest with sparkly accessories. Instead of loud thump-bump music from a DJ, a full band and singer filled the stage; the dance floor was crowded, and so was the dining area. Raven stood leaning against the bar with a gin-and-tonic and a critical eye. People having a good time wasn't the only thing he saw.

Three tough-looking men stood out to him more than anything else. They wore the requisite suits and ties and looked like successful executives and all appeared to be in their early- to mid-40s. They hung around the dining area. Security? Maybe. But the more Raven saw of them having short talks with diners, requiring them to lean close to (usually) the male half of a couple, share whispers, and receive folded cash, made Raven realize their role in the nightly business. They were the ones passing the cartel's drugs to buyers and weren't concerned about passing money and baggies in the open. The more Raven watched, the more he noticed the two bartenders giving him the stink eye, too. He wasn't acting like a regular customer. They thought he was a cop. If they were waiting for him to ask for a payoff, he wouldn't have been surprised. The only way the club operated the way it did was because the club was protected by payoffs to the cops.

There was no second level overlooking the dance floor. Raven had no idea where Colonel Kovac's office might be, nor did he catch sight of the man himself. There weren't obvious heavy hitters around. The three passing drugs didn't appear armed, but it was possible they had weapons concealed. With the amount of drugs and cash on the premises, Raven knew the firepower had to be somewhere.

In other words, even if he had a clear way to confront Kovac, the club wasn't the place for it. He didn't want a fight to break out with so many innocents—regardless of if they were buying drugs or not—potentially in a crossfire. Kovac could have a small army waiting in the wings behind the stage, too.

Ah ha. Kovac's office was more than likely behind the stage. He'd have a private entrance in the back of the building, too. Raven hadn't checked for one so far. Waiting for the former colonel to either show up for work when the place was empty, or leave when the doors closed for the night, was the best way to go. If he was going to grab the man for a conversation, the time was important; so was the place.

With the matter settled for now, Raven wondered how the women were getting along back at the hotel. He finished his gin and tonic and left the bar. The bartenders watched him, but he didn't acknowledge. Let them spend the rest of the night wondering who he was or what he wanted. If any security cameras caught his face, then the colonel could spin his wheels wondering the same thing, until Raven met him face-to-face.

THE HOTEL WAS close to the M18, and had a lot of open space around it, with a few close neighbors—other businesses. Dajbabe Hill wasn't far, but getting to the top was a longer walk than Irina Vukovic wanted to make. She'd have to navigate through a cluster of trees, and the idea of walking through a small forest without a light, or anybody knowing where she was, wasn't on the table. She walked around the side of the building, through the parking lot, to the frontage road. The freeway beyond was noisy with passing cars. She stood at the edge of the frontage road, watching the freeway and enjoyed the touch of fresh air on her face. The tall lamps in the parking lot provided a low level of light and cast a lot of shadows.

When a shoe scraped the concrete behind her, she turned. Then she screamed. It was one of the men from the restaurant and he looked mean. The man was on her in a flash, grabbing her and covering her mouth. His other two buddies joined him, Dede Bizi giving her a fast examination with his cold eyes. Irina struggled, but the goon holding her held tight. Her furtive movements did nothing to break his grip.

The man dragged her across the lot to the neighboring building, which was dark and closed for the night. Bizi pushed open the door and they took her inside. The goon smacked the back of her head and her legs gave out. She hit the floor. Gasping and crying out at the same time, she tried to take note of her surroundings. The room was dark. Somebody rolled her onto her back and the last thing she saw was Bizi's big body and his tattooed right arm aiming a gun at her and then the world went black forever.

WHEN RAVEN STOPPED THE CAR, it was because the frontage road was blocked by police units. Their flashing cherry lights lit the street. A chill crept down Raven's neck as an officer waved him through the blockage. No access to the hotel unless he drove around the block to get to the front, which he started to do. The headlamps of his car lit the tarmac ahead. He drove steadily. With his left hand, he grabbed his cell phone from his jacket and called Elena.

"What's going on, Elena?"

"She's gone, Raven!"

"What happened?"

"I went to take a shower and when I got out, she was gone and then somebody heard a gunshot. Now the police. This isn't good, Raven."

Raven cursed and followed the left-hand curve of the road.

"She was seen with *us*," Elena said.

"Don't do anything till I get up there," he said.

"All right."

Raven hung up, wondering how the opposition had found them and then thought about what he saw at the nightclub. Of course. The cartel had people at *every* hotel, not only the busy ones in the main portion of the city. Who made the call, though? A desk clerk? Janitor? Too many suspects to list. Could have been anybody who saw them arrive with Irina—and they'd certainly only had Irina's picture with which to identify her. Raven had no idea how to deal with the hotel people other than setting the building on fire after he locked them in a room.

Action could wait. First, he had to confer with Elena and let Ana Gray know what happened to her asset.

18

THE PHONE BESIDE THE BED RANG AND WOKE DETECTIVE Lieutenant Stojanovic from his already fitful sleep. Beside him, his wife continued to snore. She'd long ago learned to tune out the late-night calls. He rolled onto his side and picked up the receiver. "Yes?"

"Lieutenant, we have a homicide—"

"Why are you calling me? I'm off duty and it's late."

The caller gave his rank and name; he was one of the younger detectives on the homicide squad.

"I still don't understand why you're calling."

"The victim is somebody you know, Lieutenant. The reporter. Vukovic."

The shock flashed through Stojanovic. He sat up and stuttered as he asked where and what happened. The younger detective told him where, adding, "She was shot," and the circumstances made it very much premeditated. Stojanovic didn't ask any more questions. He promised to be at the hotel shortly. He hung up the phone.

His wife woke up. "What is it?"

He didn't turn to look at her. "I have to go to a crime scene. I'll be back as soon as I can."

He left the bed to splash water on his face and get dressed. By the time he was ready to leave, his wife was snoring again. She'd long ago adjusted to the after-midnight calls and his need to visit a crime scene when called. She didn't point out he was off duty, though. He wondered why she didn't argue.

Stojanovic arrived at the crime scene and parked outside the closure. His legs shook as he left the car, and he carried his cell phone in his left hand. This was the murder Anton Vercuni advised of. The cartel operative would soon call again to tell him what else was required. He reached the crime scene tape blocking access to the building where the murder occurred. Lights had been set up; they were bright, the night was cold, and there were a ton of cops standing around. The coroner and crime scene crew worked inside the building. Stojanovic watched from behind the crime scene tape. His expression was flat. He looked like a man standing at the edge of a cliff and thinking about jumping.

The young detective who phoned him tapped him on the shoulder. With a start, Stojanovic turned to face him.

"What do you have so far?" the lieutenant said. He straightened and cleared his throat, trying to push his reaction into a mental corner where it wouldn't seem obvious.

"It looks like the victim was dragged in here from over there," the young detective said, pointing. Stojanovic didn't look where the young man indicated. "The killers forced the lock on the door to this building and being inside, muffled the gunshot. It took a few moments before somebody understood what they heard. A couple of hotel staffers came out to look, and they saw the body inside."

"Suspects?"

"We're checking the parking lot cameras. There's enough

dust from the road for us to make out several shoe prints, but it's hard to tell—"

"Which belong to the killers and which belong to anybody else who's been through this lot in the last few hours."

"Yes, sir."

"All right. Where's the body?"

"Still inside."

The young man lifted the crime scene tape, and Stojanovic ducked to step under. He didn't want to disturb the crime scene or the work going on inside the building, so he stayed a few feet from the door. It was a good enough view. They'd put a cover over Irina Vukovic's body, and he didn't need to see her face. If the crew on-scene had identified her, it was enough for him. His left hand began to cramp. He looked at the cell phone. No call yet. He put the phone in his left pocket. Vercuni would call when he determined the time was right. There was no need to wait like a child on Christmas Eve waiting for Santa.

Stojanovic hung around for an hour, then said goodbye to the detective who summoned him and made his way back to his car. Before he started the engine, his cell rang. Stojanovic hurried to get the phone out of his pocket. He didn't have to look at the caller ID.

"What is it?"

"You're awake?" said Anton Vercuni.

"I'm at the crime scene. Talk."

"By now you know who the victim is, right?"

Stojanovic squeezed the cell phone a little too hard because he imagined it was Vercuni's neck.

"I do."

"We need a deep dive on her background. Dig into her past. Find out who she's been taking instructions from."

"The newspaper. Is it that hard for you?"

"She was doing more than working for a newspaper, Detective. We believe another hand directed her to try and find out the identity of our new boss, and we want to know who."

"What if it turns out it's only the newspaper? Seriously, Anton, this is a waste of time. It was a waste of a life."

"We wouldn't have ordered this if we didn't know we were right."

"You assume you're right."

"You're in no position to argue with me, Detective. I want the deep dive into her background. I want to know who's on her phone, her computer; all of it. She was taking instructions from an outside party. Find the person giving the orders."

"You sound like you think she was a spy of some sort."

"Some sort, indeed, Detective."

Stojanovic didn't know how to respond. In his dealings with Irina over the years, he never thought she was more than she represented. What Vercuni suggested was…a double life. More than met the eye. If it was true, Irina was the best spy on the planet. Not even a trained cop noticed she was more than she claimed.

And she reminded him of his daughter.

Bile burned in his stomach.

"Do you understand me, Detective?"

"It's not my case. I don't have any authority to get involved."

"You'll find a way. You always find a way."

Vercuni hung up. The cell phone beeped. Stojanovic dropped the phone in his lap and slammed a fist on the steering wheel, his face twisted with anger. He stifled the string of curses he wanted to scream. Doing so would only attract attention from his colleagues, and he didn't need them coming over to see if he was okay.

It was well after three a.m. Stojanovic started the engine and drove away. He had to try and get some rest before his workday began at nine. He had to maintain the "all was well" appearance for his wife. He didn't need her asking questions, either.

"Do we leave?" Elena asked.

Raven shook his head. "No, let's stay here till they're gone. I thought we could slip away, but they're everywhere. We won't get halfway to the car before they stop us."

Raven stood with his hands on his hips in Elena's hotel room, frowning; she stood nearby with a panicked look on her face.

"I didn't think she would leave, Raven. I never would have—"

"It's not your fault."

"I scared her, is what I did."

"It's not your fault," Raven repeated.

"Then whose fault is it?"

"Mine."

Elena, stunned, said nothing more, but she saw the guilt on his face and he avoided her gaze.

"I should have expected the cartel would have every hotel covered."

"What were we supposed to do? Sleep on the street?"

Raven shook his head. "No alternative I can think of keeps us from getting to this same point," he admitted.

"What if they question us?"

Raven shrugged. "What can we tell them? She was a friend of ours; it was late, she decided to share the room with you for the night. She went for a walk on her own, and this horrible event took place. We won't be suspects."

"I don't care if we're suspects or not," Elena said. "I don't want to spend any time with the police. *None*, Raven."

Now he looked at her. "We don't have a choice."

When two detectives finally knocked on Elena's door, Raven told her to sit tight. He answered. The two detectives identified themselves and Raven invited them into the room. The young officers took notice of their stressful state and explained they were there because the hotel staff had seen them with the murder victim. Raven said simply, "She was a friend of ours." After offering their condolences, the detectives took turns asking questions but never took an aggressive tone. Raven gave them the rundown he'd worked out with Elena, who nodded when one of the cops glanced at her. Irina was a friend, Raven said, it was late, she decided to sleep in the room rather than drive all the way home. How did you know the victim? The three of us met at university, my girlfriend and I are visiting Montenegro, and Irina took us around a few places. Raven named some local attractions to make the story sound better, and hoped the cops didn't ask to see any pictures or souvenirs as proof. They didn't.

When asked, Raven told the detectives the truth about where he lived. A houseboat in Stockholm. He worked as a handyman at the harbor. Elena gave Ana Gray's address in London and claimed to work as an executive assistant. With a little fudging, Raven realized she wasn't entirely lying. But these details brought up questions about the state of their relationship. Why such a long distance between the two of you? Elena said her work took her to Stockholm several weeks at a time. When the detectives finally departed, Elena sat on her bed and let out an exasperated sigh. Raven sat next to her. She looked at him with fear in her eyes.

"Now what?"

"We tell Ana. And we get ready to hit back harder than

they hit us. We start with Kovac, and then I'd like to send a message to the Vercunis."

"I'll put the stamp on the letter."

"Tell Ana we're going to need more weapons."

"Me?"

"No, I'll tell her," Raven decided. "I'll take the heat on this one."

"This isn't fair! She was the lucky one. Why couldn't it have been me?"

"Don't torture yourself, Elena," Raven said. He rose and made for the connecting door. "Try to get some rest. I'll call Ana now. We start later this afternoon."

"And in the meantime?"

Raven shrugged. "Punt." He opened the connecting door and re-entered his room. The door shut quietly behind him. Leaning against the door on the other side, Raven gave himself a moment. He'd managed to keep a lot of people alive over the years, but those he failed weighed on him. And he'd learned long ago there was no sense in grieving and wailing. Nothing mattered but striking back. Show the enemy that making him angry was the worst decision they ever made. Raven intended to show Kovac and the Vercunis and Irina's killers and anybody else from the Balkan Cartel the meaning of *payback*.

19

THE LAST COUPLE OF HOURS BEFORE OPENING FOR THE DAY
were the best for Peter Kovac, former army colonel turned
nightclub entrepreneur. As he sat in his office, located
behind the main stage, he studied the latest financial state-
ments. The club was doing well enough he wanted to bring
in some bigger names for the floor show once the current act
fulfilled their contract. The band and singer were doing well,
but it would be a major boost to get bigger names; show the
city KOVAC'S was the club to attend. He'd have to tell the
drug runners to scale back a little, not make their work so
obvious. Of course, he reflected, their activity had never
caused any trouble before, and the cops stayed paid off. He'd
reconsider the decision later. For now, all the news was good
news.

Kovac was one of Anton Vercuni's "satellite crews"—
members of the cartel who worked on the periphery. Word
reached the satellite crews within hours of the fate of the
reporter; she would no longer be a nuisance. What he
remained concerned about, though he was in no position to
bring up the subject, was the disaster in the Albanian forest.

The destruction of a major cartel facility should have been the primary topic of any discussion, but Kovac was low enough on the totem pole he probably didn't need to know what was happening. He only hoped whoever blew up the compound didn't show up at his club.

He checked his watch. Time for his inspection before the wait staff began taking chairs down from tables. He also wanted to make sure a few issues with the sound system—line static, he'd been told—had been corrected. He didn't want any problems with the evening's show. His customers hadn't complained the previous night, but he didn't want the issue to become a trend.

He left his office and wandered out onto the stage. A cleaning crew was waxing the dance floor, and their machinery made a racket—like the sounds of several vacuum cleaners going at once. The bartenders wiped the countertop and took inventory on the shelved bottles. One climbed a short ladder to get to the top shelf bottles, and Kovac hoped he didn't lose his balance. He didn't want to have an accident.

Kovac took the long way around the dance floor and conferred briefly with the bartenders; his head waiter came out from the kitchen, and Kovac shared a few words with him, too. It was an easy day so far; the chef's special sounded good, and Kovac decided he'd try some of it for dinner. He planned to stay for at least the first show of the evening to make sure the sound crew resolved the technical problems, and a short chat with the sound director assured him the problem was fixed and would not be returning. With his rounds finished and confident in the work and dedication of his staff, Kovac went the long way around the dance floor again, slipped backstage, and returned to his office. He didn't make it through the doorway, because he stopped short. Another man sat at his desk. Kovac didn't raise an alarm because the man behind the desk was pointing a gun at his belly. Then a woman came up behind him and stuck another gun in his back.

"Let's go in and talk," the woman said. "If you're good, we won't kill you."

Kovac said, "Define good."

The woman nudged him forward. He went into the office. The woman closed the door.

———

KOVAC WATCHED the man behind the desk. He was the one in charge, the one staring at him, and the one Kovac decided he'd talk to. The woman was backup. She stayed behind him, out of sight of his peripheral vision, but he knew she was there. Holding the gun. If he tried anything, she'd shoot first. Her partner would have to get out of the way, though. No, he decided, they weren't going to shoot. The guns were meant only for intimidation.

"Good afternoon, Mr. Kovac," the man said.

"You have me at a disadvantage," the nightclub owner said. "Who are you?"

The man set his gun on the desktop. He leaned forward, acting like he was the one in charge of the club, acting like the office was as familiar to him as his own bedroom. Kovac didn't like the man's attitude but kept his cool.

"Who I am isn't important," the man said. He had a deep voice and an American accent. Kovac noted the details. "Who I represent is important, but his identity will remain classified for now."

"What is this about?"

"Changes. Progress. Fresh blood. Know what I mean?"

"You still have my at a disadvantage."

"What don't you understand?"

"Anything you're talking about."

The man laughed, and so did the woman. Kovac was tempted to turn and look at her but kept his eyes on the man behind the desk.

"There's been a recent shakeup in the cartel, right?" the man said. "Get ready for another one. My lady and I represent a new boss coming into town, and you can be part of the new regime, or die with the old one. Do you understand me now?"

"Wait—"

"This town is going to start heating up, Kovac. And by the way? We aren't happy with the murder last night. There was no reason to kill Irina Vukovic. We may need to take a scalp or two for compensation, get me?"

"You mean—"

"I mean I'm going to kill one of your people," the man said, "when the opportunity strikes."

"Why are you telling me this? I'm not—"

"No, you're not a big deal. But you have the ear of a man who is, a man who is smart enough to know an opportunity when he sees one. Tell Anton Vercuni he needs to contact me."

The man picked up a pen and scribbled a contact number on one of the financial forms Kovac had studied earlier. The man stopped writing, frowned at the paper, and examined it and the others on the desk.

"You're doing pretty well, Kovac," he said. "You can do well with us if you're smart."

The man rose from the desk, picking up his gun as he stood, and slipped the gun under his jacket.

"Wanna step out of the way?"

Kovac moved aside. The man reached the door first and held it for the woman, who'd already put away her gun. Both of them went out. The door shut.

Kovac let out a breath and let his body shake as the pressure wore off. He stumbled into his seat and started moving papers around until he found his cell phone. Dialing Anton Vercuni's number, he tried to catch his breath before Anton answered. He had no idea how he was going to explain the confrontation. And how did the pair get past his security? He had to check on his guards!

"THIS IS CRAZY," Elena said.

"Let's see if the bug Ana's contact gave us is working."

Raven used an app on his phone to tune in to the electronic listening device he'd planted in Kovac's office. He hadn't placed it under the desk because it was too obvious a place for such a device. The cluttered shelving behind the desk, containing books and other random items, was better suited. Raven stuck the bug in the sliver of space behind the rear edge of a shelf and the back wall.

Kovac's frantic phone call came in loud and clear.

"I don't know who they are or where they came from but they said you shouldn't have killed the reporter and they're moving into the city. The man was American. The woman sounded European." A pause. *"Anton, why? Why do you care what she looked like..."*

ANTON VERCUNI SAID, "An American male and a European woman? Peter, tell me what the woman looked like?"

"Anton, why? Why do you care what the woman looked like? There's another party trying to take over the cartel. We have to tell the boss."

"You let me worry about the boss, Peter, and tell me what the damn woman looked like!"

Kovac did his best, admitting he hadn't seen much of the

woman, only a glimpse. Anton asked questions about her appearance Kovac couldn't answer. His only solid reply was about her voice.

"It's her," Anton said. "I'm sure it's her."

"It's *who?*" Kovac said. "Dammit, Anton—"

"The woman we caught spying here at the house. The woman we sent to the Albanian camp. The man was American? What did he look like?"

Kovac had a much better description of the male half of the pair, but Anton didn't recognize any of the features Kovac pointed out.

"Has to be him, though. The commando who rescued Elena."

"Elena is the woman?"

"Yes. I'm positive."

"What about—"

"I guess they'll find somebody to shoot, Kovac. Maybe even you. Or me, of course. Or Melika. There are all kinds of options for them."

"They obviously want Black Ember."

"You think so? Or are they playing you?"

"What do you mean?"

"Right now, don't worry about what they want. You said this fellow scribbled something?"

"A hotel and a phone number."

"Give."

Kovac repeated the information.

"All right, Kovac, listen. I'm sending three guys to see you, and you're going to take them to this hotel and identify these people. Then I want you to vanish for a week or so."

Kovac didn't hesitate. "All right. I'll be expecting them."

"I'm erasing these two," Anton said, "and if they really represent another syndicate, they're going to have to send somebody better."

"You could start a war."

"Right now," Anton said, "I want to send a message. Don't leave the club. My people will be there shortly."

ANOTHER HOTEL ROOM, this time downtown, and Raven was busy placing small bombs around the room.

"I thought you had rules about this sort of thing," Elena said, watching.

"These are only flash-bangs," he said. "They won't do any real damage. But they'll scare the hell out of whoever comes into the room."

"And you think—"

"Oh, they'll come," Raven said. He placed the last charge under a table. "It might be a while but they'll be here. Sometime tonight, I'd think."

"What do we do till then?"

"Prepare the other toys Ana sent us. We'll give them a greeting they'll never forget. The ones who survive, anyway."

After dark, when the street was still busy with traffic and pedestrians, Raven and Elena hid in the alley across the street. They dressed in old clothes purchased from a thrift store to help with their homeless appearance. Raven wasn't sure the camouflage was effective, but nobody gave them a second look as they passed the alley.

They had a nice view of the front of the hotel, and Raven hoped the cartel crew didn't show up until the street traffic cleared out. There was no telling, though. If they came to kill, they might wait; then again, there was no guarantee. But getting stuck in traffic when you needed a fast getaway wasn't on the agenda for any killer, cartel or otherwise. Raven had a feeling they'd wait.

He rigged the flash-bangs in the hotel room for remote

detonation, and Ana had supplied a motion sensor he also placed in the room. When the door opened, Raven's phone would signal the intrusion, and he'd activate the detonator. Then they'd wait. When the crew came back down, should the street be empty enough for a fight, Raven planned to give them a show. He wondered if Kovac would be among the team. The Vercunis would want him to identify him and Elena. He also wondered if the three he'd tangled with at the restaurant would be sent as well. Raven had a score to settle with them. Their heads on a spike would only be the beginning. Raven was going to burn the entire cartel to the ground. He had a plan for the Vercunis next, if Kovac played his role.

They waited some more. The street traffic faded. Hours passed. And then the gun crew showed up.

20

THE CAR STOPPED IN FRONT OF THE HOTEL, AND KOVAC climbed out with three familiar faces. It was after midnight, Raven and Elena were cramped from hiding in the alley and playing homeless, and she nudged him awake with an elbow. He shifted to be ready to fight, but kept his Uzi hidden. Streetlamps lit the faces of Kovac and Dede Bizi and Bizi's two helpers—the men he'd fought in the other alley the day before. They entered the hotel, and Raven looked at his phone. The ap showed no intrusion to his room yet. *Yet.*

The window of their hotel room overlooked the street. He expected to see the flashing strobes of the bombs he'd planted spill through the glass, and maybe the shock waves from the detonations would break the glass. It took a few minutes, and then the ap on Raven's phone signaled people other than those who belonged in the room had entered. How they overcame the electronic lock on the door, Raven only had a few ideas. The technology to spoof a key card existed and wouldn't be difficult for Bizi to acquire.

Raven traded the phone for the remote detonator and pressed the button.

The flash-bangs went off, muffled sounds of *whump*, *whump*, *whump*, as each grenade went off reaching the street. Neither Raven nor Elena heard the commotion inside as Kovac, Bizi, and the other two reacted to the auditory and sensory assault, but Raven grinned imagining their faces. They'd be down faster than it had taken to go up. Raven and Elena uncovered their weapons and prepared their response.

DEDE BIZI DIDN'T LIKE the soft-around-the-middle nightclub owner tagging along with them. He wanted to be rid of the commando and the spy once and for all and didn't want the nightclub dude as a witness. Nor did he need Kovac to "identify" the man and woman. Bizi knew quite well who they were. The only new wrinkle in the caper was the dude telling Kovac they represented parties who wanted to move into the territory. Bizi wasn't surprised. With the "change in leadership" of the Balkan Cartel, there were vultures aplenty, and it confirmed, at least for him, the commando and the spy weren't a pair of rogue law enforcement or intelligence officers operating off the books. They knew *something* now about who they belonged to, but not who sent them. Whacking the reporter was a good start at finding who sent them, but a gamble just the same. Bizi wasn't convinced the reporter was part of the problem, considering her past work, but Anton insisted, and Bizi followed orders. In the meantime, Bizi was happy to whack the other two and get them off the stage. Whoever sent them would try again, and in the process reveal more about their identities and end goals.

The elevator doors slid open and Kovac started out. Bizi grabbed his shoulder to stop him and took the lead instead. He also didn't like this hotel business; it was easily a trap, and Bizi wanted to see the signs before they went too far. But the hallway was clear and quiet. He gestured for the others to follow. Kovac walked behind him, with Rok and Milos picking up the rear.

Milos had the gear to trick the hotel room's lock into thinking somebody swiped a card, but Bizi wanted to try knocking first. Because, duh, sometimes the person you wanted was inside the room. He knocked, put his ear to the wood, knocked again. No answer. It was silent inside, not even the television made any noise.

The hotel room door had a slot above the knob, and Milos inserted a strip into the slot and used a device to run through a series of signals to find which one the lock responded to. When the lock clicked, Bizi and Rok took out their handguns. Kovac had no weapon. His job was to say, "there they are," and nothing more. Bizi hoped the former military man still had the stomach for blood spatter; if not, he'd become a headache fast, and because of his rank in Anton's organization, Bizi couldn't dump his body somewhere if the headache became more than he wanted to tolerate even for a short period.

The door was heavy. Bizi gave it a good shove and stepped through the doorway with his gun out. The lights were on, and he saw nobody inside. Rok broke off to search the bathroom; Milos looked in the closet; Kovac stood in the doorway and looked dumb.

"Find a place to sit and we'll wait," Bizi told the club owner.

The first bang made Bizi flinch. The following flash blinded him, and he screamed. More booms. More flashes. More screaming. Kovac screamed from the doorway, covering his eyes with one arm, staggering away to bump into the wall behind him. Bizi and his men crashed into each other and the walls, and it was *thud, thud, thud* until Rok knocked his head against the edge of the open door and the door slammed shut. Bizi and Rok fought over who'd twist the doorknob to get them out, and they smacked at each other, eyes shut, going by feel, until Bizi finally shoved Rok away and opened the door. The three men spilled into the hallway for more thudding against the wall, and against Kovac. Bizi had spots in his eyes. Big spots. It hurt to keep them open, so he shut them and tried not to yell. The effort didn't do much good, because Milos was shouting, "I'm blind!" and if Bizi could see him, he'd have smacked him, and he didn't want to strike out blindly and hit anybody else by mistake. They'd only end up fighting each other.

"You ain't blind, you big dummy!" Bizi yelled back instead and started feeling his way along the wall back to the elevator. They had to get out of there. They'd already made too much noise, never mind the bombs, and the hotel would be crawling with cops any second. He also didn't need witnesses. How do you whack an entire floor of a hotel to keep people quiet? And do you whack the rest of the employees after for the same reason? They hadn't brought enough ammunition to shoot so many people. It was better to simply abandon ship and get out of there.

It had been a trap, all right.

A very clever trap indeed. A big middle finger to the cartel from alleged "outside players" who wanted to take over the territory.

21

RAVEN CHECKED HIS WATCH. BIZI AND HIS CREW WERE TAKING much longer than he counted on.

"Where are they?" Elena asked.

"Patience," he said.

When they finally emerged from the hotel entrance, Bizi silent, Kovac and the other two moaning and groaning, Raven said, "It's time," and tucked the Uzi into his shoulder. He was propped on a stack of cardboard taken from a dumpster behind him, Elena in the alcove opposite. His Uzi wore the silencer he'd used in Albania, but Elena's weapon had no suppression. The enemy would think they only had one gun firing on them.

Raven waited till they were close to their car, away from the glass doors of the hotel entrance. He wanted the brick wall beside the door as their backstop. There was no sense having bullets penetrate their bodies and going through the glass. When they reached the car, he pulled the trigger and let the Uzi recoil into his shoulder. The suppressed salvo crossed the empty street and zeroed in on Bizi and his men.

The salvo smacked into the back of one of Bizi's goons as

he struggled to open the back passenger door on the driver's side. The slugs chewed up his legs and worked their way to his spine. His scream filled the night, but it was a short scream as the last of the salvo entered his back and made his heart explode. His body slammed against the car and fell onto the street.

Raven shifted his aim as Kovac and Bizi scrambled over the hood and around the car to the sidewalk side. They dropped low, but Bizi's other gunner started firing over the roof, blind shots, rounds whining off the alley wall but coming nowhere near Raven or Elena. This time, Elena took the shot. Her Uzi stuttered loudly, but her burst fell short, tearing into the body of the car and spiderwebbing side windows.

The gunner ducked out of sight. The car's interior light came on as Bizi or Kovac opened the passenger side door. Raven fired into the driver's door, his rounds punching into the metal, but not through it. Somebody managed to get behind the wheel and start the motor. Raven shot out more of the driver's side window glass. The gunner in the back seat fired through the remnants of the rear passenger side glass, and then the car peeled away from the curb and Raven jumped up and ran into the street.

Raven stopped on the median, shouldered the Uzi, and fired again at the fleeing car. Hits sparked off the rear, punched through the back glass, and scored. As the gunner in the back seat swung his weapon over the headrest to fire, he also exposed part of his head. Two of Raven's rounds found his forehead and cored his skull through and through. He only saw the man's head fall out of sight. By the time he had the slack taken up to fire again, the speeding car made a left turn. Tires screeched. For a moment, it appeared the driver might lose control, but the car survived the turn and kept going.

Raven ran back to Elena, who was on her feet and wait-ing. They ran down the length of the alley to the opposite side where their car waited. He'd managed a little payback for what happened to Irina Vukovic, but it was only the start. Next on his list was Anton Vercuni himself. And his wife, Melika.

ELENA SLAMMED the brake pedal to the floor as the big van screeched to a halt in front of them. The side doors opened and six men with submachine guns jumped out.

Raven twisted around in his seat. Another van halted behind them, the side doors opened, and another six men with submachine guns jumped out. They all wore black, including facemasks leaving only their eyes and mouths visi-ble. But none started shooting. Elena, breathing hard behind the wheel, was already sweating; Raven said, "Take it easy."

"Are you not seeing—".

"They aren't shooting, Elena, take a deep breath."

Raven faced front again. No shooting, no orders to exit the car. Raven made eye contact with the gunman closest to the front bumper and shrugged. He powered down the passenger window and yelled, "What do you want?"

Another man emerged from the van, from the passenger seat. He wasn't dressed in black and didn't carry a weapon. Instead, he was overdressed in a suit and tie. He came around the front of his men and, leaving his hands at his sides, said, "Code yellow, Mr. Raven."

"Code yellow," Raven repeated.

"Ana!" Elena said.

"Miss Gray sent me, Mr. Raven," the man continued. "We need to have a talk. Will you follow us, please?"

"Quite a crew you have," Raven said.

"I decided only an overwhelming force could keep you from going for your weapons," the man in the suit said.

"What's your name?"

"My name is Kemal Hasanaj, and Irina Vukovic was a friend of mine."

"Lead the way," Raven said. "We'll stay with you."

The man nodded and returned to the passenger seat of the van. His gunmen returned to the vehicles too. The driver of the lead van straightened the vehicle and started forward. Elena followed.

"Who is this guy?" she said.

"Somebody Ana has kept in the background and didn't tell us about," Raven said. "She's always keeping things in the background."

"Until we need them."

"You give her too much credit," Raven said. "I'm surprised her little chess moves don't get more of her own people killed."

The second van stayed behind them, keeping close. Raven went for his .45 and held it in his lap.

"If this goes south," Elena said, "your pistol won't make a difference."

"I'll take one or two of them with me, Elena," Raven said. "It's enough of a trade to make it worthwhile."

Elena followed Hasanaj's van without further reply.

22

THEY DROVE TWENTY MINUTES OUTSIDE THE CITY TO A secluded two-story house surrounded by a wooden fence. The gunners piled out of the vans and went to hide in the shadows, while Kemal Hasanaj guided Raven and Elena inside. They brought their weapons, and Hasanaj did not object. Inside, it was warm and comfortable and very well furnished, but not lived in. The place was too clean to ever have had occupants for a long period. Hasanaj led them into the living room and offered to make drinks. Raven and Elena said no, for now. Raven added, "We'd like to sort out a few questions first."

"Ask away."

Raven kept the .45 holstered and under his jacket. They set the heavier weapons in the corner and joined Hasanaj at the living room dining table near the connecting doorway to the kitchen. Raven and Elena sat across from him.

"Who are you?" Raven asked.

"I'm a smuggler Ana employs from time to time," Hasanaj said. "The rest of my days are spent running my tailoring business."

"You wear your work?"

"Best form of advertising, yes."

"Let's hear your side of this," Raven said. "I'm sure Ana told you about ours."

"I'd been assisting Irina. I can't let what happened to her go unpunished. Instead of staying in the background, it's now time for me to step forward. Be more aggressive. Everything I should have been at the beginning, but we were gathering facts, not engaging in direct-action."

"And then I came along."

"Yes. And they killed Irina."

The three of them stopped talking and looked at each other, waiting for the next person to make a move or a statement. Hasanaj finally broke the silence. "Are you sure you two don't want a drink?"

Elena said, "I'll take one. Water."

Raven nodded. Hasanaj left the table to go through to the kitchen and returned with two bottles of water and a bottle of beer for himself. "You probably aren't in the mood for anything stronger right now."

Raven and Elena twisted the caps off the bottles and drank a little. Yeah, sitting in the alley for hours and then having a gun fight didn't leave him, or Elena, in the mood got a gin and tonic.

"I helped Irina arrange meetings with connections within the cartel," Hasanaj said. "Two of them were promptly snuffed out, and the same killers threatened her—"

"We know this," Raven told him.

"Smugglers have a gentleman's agreement. We don't mess with each other. I know plenty about the Balkan Cartel and their operations. Every now and then somebody violates the agreement, but they're dealt with—swiftly. It's not often a problem."

"What are you getting at, Kemal?" Raven said.

The smuggler frowned but drank some more instead of responding with the same skeptical irritation as his guest. Raven did it for a reason. He didn't trust this new player. Raven wanted Ana's endorsement first. The fact he knew Elena's "yellow" code was a plus in his favor, but Ana held back information about Hasanaj and he wanted to know her reason.

"Wait a minute," the smuggler said. He set his beer on the table and left the room once more.

Elena turned to Raven. "I can't tell if—"

Raven held up a hand. She stopped talking.

Hasanaj returned holding a leather folder. He passed it to Raven. Elena scooted her chair closer to see what was inside.

Raven passed the pages and photos within the folder to Elena after he examined each. Every page and photo high-lighted an aspect of the cartel's business. Places of distribution, manufacture; training camps; homes of various high-level associates. Front companies. Individual soldiers and their names, crime, locations. It was a gold mine of intelligence and enough to cripple the cartel if properly used by a dedicated commando unit.

But the information did nothing to solve the mystery of who now led the cartel, and whether it was The Wolf.

"What's missing?" Raven asked. Beside him, Elena continued examining the evidence with careful attention. "And why?"

"The major piece," Hasanaj said. "The new cartel leader, of course. We know what they have in mind with the new synthetic drug, this Black Ember, as they call it, but we can't confirm the identity or the location of the man in charge."

"And nobody on the inside is talking?"

Hasanaj shook his head. "The outer layer of the cartel is as in the dark as everybody else."

"Uh-huh."

"And there's more than a synthetic drug on the cartel's agenda," Hasanaj said. "Something even worse."

"Which is?"

"The proceeds from the new drug will fund a private army. They want to increase the size of the cartel's fighting force and take over Serbia and make it a haven for terrorists, criminals, anybody in violation of international law who needs sanctuary and can pay their prices."

"And you've known this for how long?"

"Long enough."

"Did Ana know?"

"She's not the only one who keeps secrets until the time is right."

"You mean before I showed up and started burning compounds in Albania."

Hasanaj nodded.

"And what else?"

"I liked Irina very much."

"Maybe if we'd had this a little earlier—" This time, Elena silenced Raven. She did so with a hand on his leg, under the table, and a shake of her head. Raven took a breath and said, "Anton Vercuni. He's the primary representative of the cartel in Podgorica. He *must* know where the new boss is hiding. And his name?"

Elena said, "I was looking for those details when they caught me."

"He's our next stop. Our stunt tonight will hopefully draw Vercuni and his cronies into one place to talk about it. We need to be there when it happens."

"I know where he is," Elena said.

"And my people will be at your disposal," Hasanaj added.

"They appear capable," Raven said. "Is this place yours?"

"No, it's one of Ana's safehouses. You're welcome to stay."

"We should at least stay tonight," Raven said. "Tomorrow will be another busy day."

23

ANTON VERCUNI STOOD UNDER THE PORCH OVERHANG watching the cars arrive.

He'd called the meeting of his sub-lieutenants after the debacle the night before, when Bizi and Kovac were almost killed and Bizi lost the two men he hired to deal with their current problem. So far, the only redeeming thing about losing the two hired guns was Anton didn't have to pay them. Saving the money did no good, though; such a small amount was minuscule, and hardly protected him from whoever the man and woman—the commando and the spy, as Bizi had decided to call them—represented.

Before Anton took his problem to The Wolf, which he didn't want to do, although he assumed The Wolf *already* knew what was happening, he wanted to bring in his officers and generals to let them know the score and get their suggestions. Anton decided, after coming up with several less-good alternatives, a larger army had a better hope of eliminating the commando and the spy than Bizi and his selected gunners. Bizi had succeeded in killing the reporter, however; if the corrupt cop, Stojanovic, did his job, more answers were forthcoming as to who was responsible for the late unpleasantness.

The three cars rounded the top of his sloped, curving driveway connecting the house to a gate and the main road. Anton and his wife lived in a large spread, covering two acres, and their neighbors occupied other hillsides and hilltops nearby, but not so close you could see through the windows. They had decent privacy, with tall trees adding to the cement wall blocking visual and physical access. The blockage also aided in making sure nobody saw the armed force Anton kept around. One of the neighbors could examine everything through binoculars, if he or she were so inclined, but nobody would. The folks who lived in these hills liked their privacy, and didn't intrude on anybody else's either.

The cars parked one beside the other at the front of the house, and Anton smiled as doors opened and people climbed out. There was only one woman among the group.

Bako Simovic buttoned his blazer and squared his shoulders as he walked around the front of his Mercedes sedan. His driver and two bodyguards also exited and waited by the car for orders. Bako was wiry, almost gaunt, in his late 30s, his thinner hair slicked back with too much gel. His tight slacks made his legs look skinny.

Savan Kalezic emerged from the middle car. He was the oldest of the three sub-lieutenants, in his early forties, and the tallest. A retired boxer, he was still thick, but wider now too, with none of the fighter's physique he'd once possessed. His thick neck looked flabby, his middle bulge gave away his sedentary lifestyle, and his loud yellow suit did nothing to lessen the impact of Sevan being somebody past his prime and out of his time. But he was a good earner who ran a distribution crew who made sure Anton, and, of course, the cartel's product reached the users who demanded it, within and outside of Montenegro.

Petra Carapic slinked out of the last car, and Anton smiled hoping Melika didn't see him staring at her. Mid-thirties, with a lean athletic build and long legs, Petra entered a room and made every other woman disappear. Sharp cheekbones, full lips, piercing green eyes; all of those features drew the kind of attention she liked, and she reserved a cold stare for the kind of attention she didn't like, a stare known to send men scrambling for cover. She wore dark jeans and leather boots and a fitted jacket Anton knew concealed both a pistol and a knife. She was a knife fan, too, but not as big of a collector as he.

More armed bodyguards followed Petra and Sevan, and it was Bako who said, "Where do we station our men?"

As if on cue, the head of house security appeared from around the corner, coming up on Anton's right. Anton introduced the man and told the bodyguards to report to him for their duty stations. He reminded everybody this was a friendly meeting but they should be on guard for reasons they'd soon discuss.

"I've been hearing rumors," Petra said with her thick accent, "and I don't like what I'm hearing, Anton."

"Reality is worse than rumor," Anton told her. "Come along inside. Melika has food and drinks waiting."

"I'm watching my weight," Petra announced, "so I will skip my usual six drinks and only consume three." She walked past Anton to enter the house before he led them inside. Anton gestured for the two men to follow her, grinning, and picked up the rear. Petra's boots tapped on the hardwood floor as they headed for the back patio.

"I'll take the drinks Petra skips," announced Savan, slapping Anton on the back.

Anton was glad they were in such a good mood, but wondered how long their attitude would last when he gave them the full rundown. There was only one way to find out…

MELIKA WAITED in the dining room with Peter Kovac.

Anton insisted Kovac join the meeting to testify to what happened at the nightclub and the hotel. Dede Bizi wasn't there; he was on the street, hunting.

The dining room contained an example of what unlimited funds provided; its high ceilings adorned with a crystal chandelier casting prismatic glints across polished mahogany walls. In the center sat an expansive, hand-carved rosewood table, the shape of which Melika had drawn herself, inlaid with mother-of-pearl. The table's surface gleamed under the soft glow of gilded candelabras. Heavy damask drapes framed floor-to-ceiling windows, showing off a stone-balustraded patio balcony. On the balcony, four armed men stood guard, keeping their weapons out of sight. Beyond, rolling green hillsides stretched in all directions, funneling the eye to the center of colorful Podgorica. It was a view Anton never tired of.

"Look at all this grub!" Bako exclaimed. Serving trays occupied the center of the table, a variety of food available, two servers in black and white uniforms standing nearby for drink orders. Melika greeted everyone and introduced Kovac and everyone sat. Anton's wife and Petra shared friendly but cautious glances. Melika was giving the other woman a run for the money in her blue cocktail dress and wavy black hair.

The servers took drink orders. Petra asked for a tall Aunt Roberta, and Anton stared at her with wide eyes. For somebody who wanted to cut back on her alcohol, she'd just ordered what might be the strongest cocktail ever invented.

Bako and Saran were fine with bottled beer.

Small talk filled the room while everybody settled down, Anton steering away from any other business talk. Now wasn't the time to discuss the usual problems on the street. They'd always be there, and easy to solve, at a later time. They had a bigger problem, and Anton wanted one hundred percent attention on the commando and the spy.

"Hey, Anton," Savan said, "are these windows bulletproof?"

"They better be," Bako echoed.

"You're all paranoid," Petra said. She sat with her back to the glass.

"We're safe," Anton assured them.

He opened the conversation once the drinks arrived and everybody served themselves portions of food from the center of the table.

"All right, listen up," Anton said. "We have a problem, and we need to work together to solve the problem." He went into detail of Elena Covaci attempting to infiltrate their organization and how Melika caught her spying inside the house. He told the rest of the story without excluding any detail and brought Kovac into the conversation to tell his side of the story. Kovac had the best look at the "commando" who rescued Elena Covaci, and Anton pressed him on a detailed description.

Kovac added, "They aren't law enforcement. I think they're a vanguard for somebody who wants to take over our territory."

Everybody began talking at once; Anton raised his voice and calmed the outbursts. "Speculating isn't going to help," he said. "Arguing about what to do isn't going to solve the problem."

Melika jumped in. "What we need is a strategic action plan, with all of us committing resources—"

Whatever else Melika Vercuni wanted to say, she didn't get the chance. The shooting started. And everyone seated around the table witnessed how well the glass held up.

24

A SWARM OF SHOTS SMACKED INTO THE PATIO GLASS, STRIKING with authority, gouging chunks out of the thick material but leaving behind spiderweb splatters catching everyone's attention, especially Petra's. The bullets would have hit her had the glass not stopped them, and she screamed as more slammed home and dove under the table. The others quickly joined her, Anton yelling for everyone to keep calm, but nobody listened. Another swarm of shots, the guards on the balcony reacting, drawing their weapons, and then—

Single shots, loud cracks of thunder. One guard went down, a sprawl of arms and legs. Another swam of fire smacked against the glass. Anton's body twitched and tensed with each impact. He knew the bullets couldn't penetrate the glass, but what if? It wasn't like he'd tested the glass himself. The installers told them it was what he wanted; he signed the papers; they did the work. For years the glass had only needed cleaning every week. Nobody had ever tried shooting at it before. But now, as it stood up to the constant barrage, he decided the expense, a lot at the time, had been worth it. Too bad his guards were dropping like bowling pins, not even able to get off any return fire. Another crack, another one down. The two not shot took cover behind the balcony wall. It wasn't very high, but at least it shielded them from the sniper.

The front doors slammed open and the house guard and the rest of the force ran into the room. Anton started yelling for everybody to evacuate to another room, and he noticed everybody jerk and jump each time another bullet struck. Now the sniper with the big rifle was shooting, the shots hitting harder, making the window vibrate. The chandeliers rocked back and forth as the vibrations shook the ceiling, too. Anton didn't know what was hitting the glass, but it was heavy-duty indeed, and if it kept up, who knew if the glass would break? He and Melika ushered everybody out, fast, and Anton noticed Petra paused long enough to grab her Aunt Roberta and down a long sip as she hurried out. She didn't spill a drop.

KEMAL HASANAJ FOUND an empty house on the hillside to the left of the Vercuni property, a rental unoccupied at present. Using a phony name and credit card, Hasanaj secured use of the home for three days. Raven and Elena made a sniper's nest in the dirt beneath the rental's balcony, which extended from the hillside, supported by thick concrete legs. Covered by the balcony overhang, none of the goons on Vercuni's balcony saw any sunlight glint of Raven's sniper scope.

Hasanaj had two men in the house with a video camera zoomed in on Vercuni's meeting. They'd look at the faces later. Raven expected the glass wouldn't shatter under the impacts of the 9mm slugs from Elena's Uzi, or his modified 7.62 M-14 rifle. But the point wasn't to kill the Vercunis or their guests. The point was to frighten them; the point was to keep up the pressure and make them run to the new boss for help. When they did, Raven and Elena wouldn't be far behind.

They watched. They waited. When the party entered the dining room, Raven wished he were inside too. The spread on the table looked really good. It would have been nice to get rid of them up close, all at once. But he rarely had such gifts handed to him.

While he watched through the sniper scope, Elena shifted, scratched, breathed hard. Raven tried to ignore it but eventually had to say something. He pulled away from the scope and turned to her.

"Are you all right?" He kept his voice low out of habit more than necessity.

She nodded, moving her head too fast. Sweat coated her forehead. She pulled a bandanna from a back pocket and tied it around her head.

"Elena?"

"I'm fine."

"You don't look fine."

"It's the bugs, okay? Bugs bother me."

"Bugs."

"Yes."

"A couple of spiders and a little lizard are bothering you?"

"We don't have time to discuss this, Raven."

"I can do this alone if you need to—"

"No!"

"All right."

"I was in there, Raven. They locked me in the basement. Anton Vercuni has a thing for knives, okay? He collects them. He wanted to cut me open and it was only Melika who stopped him."

Raven nodded.

"And I think she only stopped him because the new boss wanted me moved to Albania."

"I get it."

"Don't ask me again."

"I won't."

Raven resumed his view through the scope. He'd respect Elena's request unless her issues interfered with the mission. So far, they hadn't, but until now, they hadn't been close to the people who put her through her most recent ordeal.

And then he decided he should cut her some slack. Having faced his own traumatic moments and his own load of PTSD from them, he understood what she might be going through.

Elena presently opened the festivities. She estimated it was thirty yards to the Vercunis' balcony, and Raven didn't want any stray shots going wide. She aimed a quarter inch above the patio glass and started firing single shots. The submachine gun bucked against her shoulder but she held it tight so the muzzle didn't waver.

Raven watched the shots hit through his sniper scope, and grinned when the party around the table went for the floor. He wondered who the second woman was, the one with her back to the glass, who presented her rear end at his crosshairs. Would have been a good shot had the glass not stopped Elena's salvo.

The guards on the balcony couldn't tell where the shooting came from, and their panicked expressions as they searched in vain for the source of the gunfire almost made Raven feel bad. *Almost.* He took up slack on the M-14's trigger and sent a 7.62 slug across the space. The shot cracked and echoed through the hills, joining the firecracker-like sound from Elena's weapon. He dropped two of the guards before the last two went flat under the portion of the balcony wall facing him and Elena. They were low enough for him to be unable to see the tops of their heads over the top of the wall. He switched to the glass, his rounds tearing bigger chunks out of the glass, and still giving the occupants the shits. They finally hurried out of the room, but not before the woman with the fine posterior grabbed her drink and took a pull as she headed out. If it was a signal to him saying she wasn't afraid, he had to give her credit. She had balls, all right.

"I think we've done our job," Raven said.

"Agreed."

Raven still peered through his scope, watching the interior of the house. "I'd love to be a fly on the wall in there."

"We need to go, Raven."

"Right."

They cleared the sniper's nest and signaled Hasanaj's team to pull out.

THERE WAS a problem with their escape route.

Only one road led up and down the hillside neighborhoods, two lanes each way. And they had to pass the Vercuni house on the way down.

If Raven were in charge of the Vercuni troops, he'd want them outside and ready to take out any vehicle containing anyone who appeared armed. He and Elena and Hasanaj's two gunners rode down in the four-door sedan and tried to look natural. Raven had his own Uzi on his lap. The Hasanaj troopers were similarly armed, and Elena drove, letting the sedan glide along the road without giving the motor too much gas and only tapping the brakes now and then. She kept the speed around twenty-five to thirty, and when the road curved left she warned they were coming up on Vercuni's main gate. The car picked up speed with the downward slope, Elena braking and steering at the same time. Most of the homes were blocked from the roadway via fences, wrought-iron or otherwise, with bushes and trees filling in the gaps and making what lay beyond a mystery. Raven wasn't interested in the homes. He only wanted to make sure none of them were in the line of fire should the opposition come out and fight. And then they were speeding past the iron gate at the start of Vercuni's driveway. It was a plain gate filling the gap in the concrete wall, trees spilling over the top of the wall, further concealing the property. Raven turned his head as they passed, and then the gate swung open. The snout of the first emerging car passed through the gap, and screeched tires as it spun onto the main road.

"Here they come!"

A second black sedan turned onto the road and both grew larger as they raced to catch up with Raven and Elena. Elena pressed the accelerator now, the car surging, twisting the wheel back and forth as she navigated the curving blacktop.

Raven snapped open the Uzi's bolt and told Elena to start looking for a spot to pull off and fight. Shooting at bullet-proof glass might have spooked the major players, but they'd catch their breath and brush off the incident. So now he'd kill some of their underlings and send a further message to show them they didn't have as much protection as they thought.

The Vercuni sedans grew larger in the rearview mirror...

25

Anton Vercuni needed to seize the reins otherwise he'd look weak. He grabbed the house guard and said, "We have a chance to get them! Get a pair of crews into the cars outside. There's only one road, and they have to pass the house."

The house guard started issuing orders before the words left Anton's mouth. Four gunners didn't need any further prompting to volunteer. With each toting their own submachine gun, four piled into two of the Mercedes sedans parked out front. The cars peeled out and started down to the main gate.

Anton watched them leave and felt somebody step up beside him. Petra was there, still holding her drink.

"They better not miss," she said.

"I agree."

Anton more than hoped the gunners' aim didn't waver. If he could be rid of the problem this easily, there'd be no need to tell The Wolf anything except they'd *solved* the problem.

"All right," he said, "back inside. Let's finish the meeting. We still have to talk about Black Ember. The release date isn't far away."

RAVEN UNBUCKLED his seat belt and prepared for another chance to strike back for Irina Vukovic's murder.

Hasanaj's men sat in the back seat. They'd impressed Raven so far. He only knew their first names—Aram and Lilit. Both were under five and a half feet, with dark hair and wiry frames, but they'd captured clear video of the meeting in the Vercuni house and now prepared their own weapons to join the fight. Each carried a Glock-18 machine pistol.

Aram said, "We are yours to command."

"Stay loose for now," Raven told them. He watched the Mercedes cars in the passenger side mirror, losing sight of them every few moments as Elena navigated a curve. He had no idea how many guns they faced, and he was glad to have the extra firepower Hasanaj's men provided.

The mountain road twisted some more, Raven sliding in his seat, the edge of the road ever present in his mind. The car wouldn't run off the edge and down a cliff but instead smack into one of the estate walls of the properties flashing by. He wanted to avoid such a crash, and Elena was making use of every inch of road, crossing over the median at times, keeping them on a steady downward course. The tires screeched now and then. So far, it wasn't anything Elena couldn't control.

A shot cracked behind them. The bullet slammed into the trunk. Raven hoped the camera equipment stored there wasn't damaged. But it made one thing clear. They couldn't outrun the Vercuni gunners and Elena, as yet, hadn't found a spot to pull out and make a stand. They had to fight while on the move.

"Keep it steady as you can!" Raven shouted.

Elena drifted through a curve with surgical precision and didn't raise an alarm when Raven powered down his window. He told Aram and Lilit to stay low, and with the Uzi held like a pistol in his left hand, eased half his body out the window to fire at the pursuing cars. He held the muzzle low, letting a few of the rounds go wide as the car rode over bumps and Elena made her maneuvers. Most of his salvo scored. Holes sprouted in the hood of the lead Mercedes, and the rest traced a line across the windshield. The window spiderwebbed, blocking the view of the driver. Raven fired again and emptied the Uzi, creating more cracks across the windshield. The driver missed a turn, ran off the road, and crashed into an estate wall, the car almost folding in on itself as it crumpled. Half the car remained in the roadway, and the second Mercedes swerved to miss. Raven slipped back into the car to reload, but at least now they only had one Mercedes to contend with.

"Turnout ahead!" Elena shouted as Raven locked open the Uzi's bolt.

"Brace yourselves!" Raven shouted to the men in the back seat.

Elena slammed the brakes, yanking the car into the turnout. The car skidded to a stop, road dust billowing, the scent of burned brake pads lingering in the air. The Mercedes shot past; the driver unable to duplicate the maneuver. Elena floored the accelerator and sped after the enemy car. Raven leaned out the passenger side once again, the Uzi in his right hand this time, and Lilit also leaned out the back with his own and Aram's Glock-18 machine pistol clutched in his fists.

Raven fired at the rear tires while Lilit fired on the back glass. A gunner leaned out to shoot back, and Raven's next burst clipped the side of his head. His body jerked and dropped, half of him hanging outside the car, only to fall out on the next bump. Elena swerved to avoid the body. Lilit's next pair of bursts chewed up the driver's side of the

Mercedes, and Raven noticed a splatter of blood cover the windshield inside. Elena braked hard. The Mercedes swung off the road, bumped up the shoulder, and plowed over a mailbox before crashing, like the other, into another home's exterior wall. Elena picked up speed again as they continued down the remaining length of roadway.

Hasanaj's men let out whoops of celebration, while Raven and Elena only exchanged a silent glance. She wasn't sweating anymore.

"Good shooting," Raven called to the back.

"Not as good as it could have been," Elena said.

"What do you mean?"

"If we'd been able to get them inside the house today would have been a lot different."

"You'll settle your score soon enough. Don't let rage govern your actions."

"What do you know about it?"

"More than you think, Elena."

Her hands tightened on the wheel, then loosened.

"Where to now?" she said.

"Back to the safehouse," Raven told her. He wedged the hot Uzi under his seat and hoped they were done with the gunplay for a little while.

VOJIN STOJANOVIC MADE SURE TO TAKE HIS LUNCH ON TIME and go to a corner restaurant not far from police headquarters. He sat at the counter with a hot sandwich and coffee. The counter waitress buzzed back and forth tending to the diners seated there; behind him, more activity, tables full, the loud chatter competing with the noise in the kitchen. White walls, red slashes; it was a typical diner catering to downtown workers. Stojanovic was happy to let the noise mute his thoughts. He was waiting for Anton Vercuni to make an appearance. The cartel operative phoned earlier in the morning and said he wanted to talk about the latest regarding the Vukovic homicide. The phrase turned Stojanovic's guts. The son of a bitch was behaving like he wanted to have a casual conversation about a matter he was in no way involved with. But the drug pusher had another agenda. He wanted to know what the woman's background trace revealed.

The woman. He hated referring to Irina so coldly. She was Irina Vukovic, 38, murdered by the Balkan Cartel for…what? *What* had she discovered? What knowledge put the bull's-eye on her back? Why was Anton Vercuni so obsessed with her background check and who she communicated with on her personal computer and other devices?

Vercuni made it clear he wanted to know what the police turned up. He was looking for something in her past. How was it related to why he ordered her murder?

The case was making it hard for him to sleep, and he had to force himself to eat to keep his wife from asking questions. The constant monitoring of his behavior, the effort to act natural, was taking a toll, and the lieutenant knew he had to make a drastic choice in order to bring the situation to a close. Because he also had the prying eyes of his superiors to deal with. There'd been no further conversations with his boss after the last confrontation at his desk, but Stojanovic wasn't going to start believing he was home free.

"Did you pay?"

Stojanovic looked left as Anton Vercuni slid onto the stool next to him.

"Not yet," the cop said.

"Good." The cartel operative got the waitress's attention, ordered the same as Stojanovic, and told her to add it to his bill.

The cop gave Vercuni a dirty look.

"With what I'm paying you," Vercuni said, "you can afford it."

Then Stojanovic noticed Vercuni's wife, Melika, sitting by herself at a table by the front window. She had a view of the two of them at the counter.

"Keeping you honest," Vercuni said. "And yes, she's carrying a weapon."

"I am, too," Stojanovic said.

"Good! Then all three of us will behave, won't we?"

"This could be dangerous, you know."

"Why?"

"The department is watching me."

"Really? Right now?"

Stojanovic shrugged. "Could be."

"Well, we'll give them some nice pictures, won't we?"

Stojanovic sighed and took a bite of his sandwich and chewed while Vercuni decided about getting to the point.

"Tell me what you've learned so far. Anything useful?"

"Nothing to indicate she was working for anybody except her newspaper."

"I don't believe you."

"What does it matter to me what you believe? I'm telling you what's there."

"Nothing."

"Correct," Stojanovic said. "Nothing. I don't understand why you wasted the time to kill her."

Stojanovic had two roles to play. At HQ and with his wife, he had to be the dedicated cop and husband. He had to be the opposite with Vercuni. Cold, calculated, with a "What's in it for me?" attitude. He had to act like none of this bothered him because if what he really thought and felt showed, he'd be next on Vercuni's hit list.

"What have you collected from her apartment?" The waitress brought Vercuni's sandwich and coffee. She set the plate down hard, and it scraped against the countertop, dislodging the top slice of bread from the sandwich. Vercuni put it back in place and took a bite. "Not bad," he said. "Is this your favorite here?"

"No."

Vercuni spoke with his mouth full. "The apartment. What did you find?"

Stojanovic shrugged. He didn't have to consult a list; he knew the items by heart.

"A computer, her phone—she had two, one belongs to the

newspaper—lots of papers and notebooks. Usual household items and personal things."

"What about her internet history? Emails? Those have been searched, right?"

"Maybe if you told me what you were looking for—"

"No," Vercuni said. "I want everything. I'll know it when I see it."

"Excuse me?"

"Bring me the evidence. All of it."

"You want me to bring you evidence we have locked up and cataloged?"

"Yes," Vercuni said.

"Just tell me what you're looking for. What you want isn't possible. Not even the slightest bit possible."

"You need to find a way, Lieutenant. Time is of the essence, and I need *my* people to do the digging."

"No." Stojanovic ate some more. His sandwich wasn't hot anymore; neither was his coffee. He cursed as he set the cup back down.

"You don't have a choice, Lieutenant."

"Really?"

"It would be a shame if anything happened to your wife. You know, after she recovered from her surgery and all."

"You son of a bitch."

"It would be a shame if something happened to you, too."

"Are you threatening a cop?"

"Am I? Remember, if we go down, so do you."

"Or the other way around."

"All I need is the phone or the laptop."

"You're going to ruin everything, Anton."

"The phone, then. Her personal phone. It won't be missed. The other is still there and nobody will notice because who has more than one phone?"

Stojanovic ate the last bite of his sandwich and washed it down with cold coffee.

"I can probably get one or the other," the cop said.

"Oh, so now it's not impossible?"

"I just thought of a way."

"See? Where there's a will, there's a way. I'm glad you're cooperating."

"How do you want to handle delivery?"

STOJANOVIC'S IDEA was to check out the laptop and personal phone for "outside analysis" which, he supposed, wasn't incorrect. But it was a stretch of the truth and again stirred up the acid in his gut. The charade made Vercuni happy, and as the lieutenant delivered the two items in a box, he began making his exit plan. Homicide detectives know how to get away with murder.

For Anton and Melika, a win was a win, and they didn't care how the lieutenant justified the handover. They had what they wanted, and now it was time to find what they needed.

Anton drove while Melika sat beside him. She said, "What if Stojanovic is correct and there's nothing to find?"

"We'll find it. We have to."

"Why don't you tell *me* what you're looking for. Since, you know, I'll be the one sitting in front of the screen."

"Evidence of rumors I've been hearing."

"What kind of rumors?"

"When our friends visited Kovac, they claimed to be part of another syndicate trying to muscle in, right?"

"You don't believe them."

"No, of course not. This is what I've heard, and again it's

only a rumor, but I'm pretty sure it's true. There's an independent organization, all right, but not criminal. They're *spies*. It's a freelance organization reportedly run by a lady in either Germany or Britain, and she sends out these people—"

"This is movie garbage, Anton."

"There's been enough chatter about it to make me believe it."

"I'll buy extra popcorn."

"Irina *has* to have been part of this organization, and the other two, as well," Anton said. "They aren't law enforcement. They sure as hell aren't competitors. What else can they be?"

Melika didn't have an answer and admitted so. If they eliminated the first two options, the third had to be the truth.

"We need to find out who these people are," Anton said, "and stop them at the source. Go to them. *Kill them*. Leave nothing alive after we're done."

RAVEN SAID INTO HIS PHONE, "It took you long enough to get back to me, Ana."

"My apologies. What's so urgent? Something about Irina?"

Raven stood outside the safehouse and hoped Hasanaj didn't have a long-distance microphone aimed at him. He was thirty yards from the house in an open lot with tall grass and hard-packed dirt.

"Do you know Kemal Hasanaj?"

"Yes."

"Were you ever going to tell us about him?"

"What happened, Raven?"

He explained how Hasanaj intercepted him and Elena and

their new alliance, ending with details about the hit on Vercuni's house. He made sure to point out Hasanaj was taking a greater role to avenge Irina's murder.

Ana didn't reply immediately. When she did, what she said gave Raven no confidence.

"I think you can trust him."

"What worries me," Raven said, "is why you didn't tell us about him before, and your qualifier now."

"He'd been working with Irina, and he's done a lot of work for me in other areas, and he's done well with every assignment. But between the two of us? I can't be sure he isn't angling for part of the Balkan Cartel's territory. Or maybe even all of it."

"Uh-huh."

"Now you know why I didn't want you to know about him right away."

"Uh-huh."

"I'm sorry about what happened to Irina," Ana said.

"What else haven't you told me?"

"Nothing."

"Are you sure?"

"He's the only detail I kept from you, Raven. I promise."

"Uh-huh. Before I took this job for you, I had another case where somebody wasn't what they claimed and tried to kill me. It got ugly. A lot of people died."

"Keep an eye on him. He could do something drastic at the last minute."

Spinou's face flashed through Raven's mind. "Like shooting me in the back."

"Just be careful. I don't want any further casualties. This has already cost us—"

"Ana?"

"Wh—what?"

"I'm getting a little tired of this, Ana."

"Okay."

"Call Elena if you need to reach us." Raven ended the call and looked mad as he walked back to the house.

27

HASANAJ SPREAD THE MAP ACROSS THE TABLE. RAVEN SHIFTED pictures and other documents out of the way. There was plenty of room, but the map took up more space than any of the other clutter on the tabletop.

They were in a warehouse, under bright fluorescent lights, in the southern part of the city. It was a property owned by Hasanaj but rarely used—except for moving contraband from one point to another. There was no contraband currently stored in the place, though, and their conversation had a slight echo within cavernous empty space. He'd left a handful of his men, all armed, at each door; others watched from parked cars outside. Raven wasn't expecting trouble, but the cartel had ways of finding people, as he'd learned the hard way. A few extra guns and a wall of defense wasn't a bad idea. He wore his pistol, too, in its usual position under his left arm. His jacket covered the shoulder harness, and he'd zipped the coat to fight off the chill inside.

The warehouse was cold and smelled of instant coffee. Hasanaj hadn't bothered installing any creature comforts in the place. A table not far from them contained the coffee maker and assorted snacks. The plumbing worked in the single bathroom, but the light didn't. They had to carry a flashlight if they needed to use it.

The tabletop contained the map, documents with details on cartel activities, surveillance photos, and pictures of the major players in the cartel—all but the new boss, of course. Raven had a plan to keep the heat on the cartel operatives they'd shook up at the Vercuni meeting. He wanted to turn up the burners, make them all unstable, uncertain, and create a need to run to the boss for orders. And he planned to be on their tails when they did.

"All right," Hasanaj said, twisting the cap off a red felt pen. "We've been over the cartel's logistics network. The video identified Vercuni's associates, which matched with what I'd already gathered. If you want to target those three next, I suggest you flip a coin and pick one."

"I want two things," Raven said. "We need to find where they're producing or preparing to distribute this new drug of theirs, the Black Ember, and I want somebody alive to ask about the new boss."

"Fair enough." Hasanaj leaned over the map. He didn't need to consult any of the documents for what he did next. "We have Bako Simovic here"—he made a red mark on the map—"who manages their safe houses. Savan Kalezic is here" —another red dot—"and he's transportation coordinator. Manages the moving of the drugs from point A to point B. Overseeing distribution is the woman, Petra Carapic, and she's here"—one last red mark—"if we take them out, it's a major blow to the cartel. Vercuni and his wife will have no choice but to get the big boss involved if they're gone."

Raven nodded. "We'll hit Bako first. Make sure the others have no place to run, and we can get to Petra and Savan after."

Hasanaj gestured to Raven's left, and Raven turned his

head. Elena sat at another table. She'd spread her weapons out, with several boxes of ammunition laying open. She stuffed rounds into magazines with shaking hands, dropping one or two, cursing, stopping to bend over and retrieve the fallen cartridges. Raven shook his head at Hasanaj. He'd deal with her later. She'd been okay during the chase after shooting up Vercuni's house, but since their return, she'd been withdrawn, with a smoldering anger brimming beneath the surface of her words and actions and facial expressions. She was a bomb ready to explode. Raven understood, but if she went too far, she'd become a liability, fast. He hoped a quiet talk with her before they left, and privately, of course, with neither Hasanaj nor his men around, would soothe her inner turmoil. He *hoped*. Combined with the escape from Albania, she was probably approaching her breaking point.

Raven returned to the topic. "We'll need Bako alive, I guess. A dead man can't answer questions."

"You can always ask the others, too," the smuggler said.

"They'll have more troops with them. I expect a tougher fight, which means I won't be trying to shoot anybody in the leg. Bako will have the knowledge. He'd be the one the boss would come to if he needs a place to hide; he'll know the boss's name."

A gust of wind outside pressed against the warehouse. The upper roof panels, corrugated metal, shuddered. One of the radios used by the security team inside crackled. The watchers sitting outside were checking in. All was well. Raven and Hasanaj refined their plan a little. Raven wanted as much backup as Hasanaj could spare, and the smuggler promised to either provide the men he needed or ask for volunteers. He had a feeling there'd be no shortage of volunteers for this fight. Taking down the Balkan Cartel...they'd do it for the fun of it, and the possibility of getting their hands on some of the spoils when the smoke cleared. Raven decided not to challenge the statement for now. But he'd make notes on who was who and where they were in case Hasanaj attempted what Ana suspected and he met them again the hard way. For now, Raven was only interested in a motivated ally.

ELENA SET another loaded magazine on the table and picked up the last empty one. She was loading the thirty-round stick mags for her Uzi, which rested on the table, smelling of fresh oil. She'd broken down the weapon and scrubbed every part before applying the lubrication.

She needed her weapon ready for the coming action. It needed to be as reliable as the mail. The weapon had served her well so far, but there was always the chance of a misfeed no matter how well maintained a weapon might have been.

She grabbed fresh rounds from the half-empty box in front of her and started pressing them into the magazine. The spring was strong, and she had to press hard.

The voices of Raven and Hasanaj weren't lost in her concentration. She heard every word. Elena didn't want to take *anybody* alive, but she understood what Raven wanted to do. She needed the answers, too, whatever Bako provided. Yes, it's The Wolf; no, it's not The Wolf. If it wasn't, would she settle down a little?

She felt the storm inside her. The bubbling anger. The rage. The bugs on her skin, their pinpricks of movement; she wanted to scream. Another mantra sprang to mind. *It's all in your head. It's not real.* But still she breathed hard and shivered from cold sweat. Or did the shiver come from something she didn't quite grasp yet?

She kept pressing rounds into the magazine and ignored her shaking hands.

I can do whatever I have to do to survive.

28

REACHING BAKO SIMOVIC REQUIRED TWO HELICOPTERS. THE cluster of safe houses where he conducted most of his day-to-day business was in the open country not far from the border with Bosnia-Herzegovina.

Hasanaj and a group of his shooters accompanied Raven and Elena on this trip, partly as a show of solidarity with Ana Gray's effort, and also to show his men he wasn't afraid to mix into the action. He'd outfitted his people with the latest and greatest in small arms and portable explosives. He'd offered to replace Raven and Elena's Uzis with weapons more powerful, but both passed. Raven liked the Israeli SMG and wasn't terribly concerned with such things as "stopping power"—the 9mm in the submachine gun format did quite well and brought down a lot of bad guys. The smugglers' crew could use the heavy weapons. They would, of course, come in handy.

The choppers landed ten miles from the complex. At least, Raven referred to it as a complex. Hasanaj described it as a cluster of home-sized structures surrounded by a wooden fence. It looked like a ranch, he added. There was certainly a grounds crew to make sure the patch of earth the cluster sat on didn't get overgrown with weeds a mile high, but they had no cattle, no crops, nothing to indicate anything happened there. Every now and then people came to stay a while. Later, they left.

The cluster was one such "sanctuary" in the cartel's chain, and the one where Bako Simovic lived and directed the operations of the other secret hideaways.

It was dark and cold. Using night vision equipment, Hasanaj and his ten shooters, along with Raven and Elena up front, made the ten-mile hike across open ground. There were dips and grooves and foothills to navigate, and natural cover existed, but there wasn't a large number of places to hide if any shooting started. There wouldn't be at the ranch, either. From the pictures Hasanaj showed him, Raven noted the huge open space between the fenced perimeter and the cluster of structures.

Raven and Elena hiked steadily, the bright moon in the clear sky providing enough illumination to keep their night vision working. Raven liked the fact there were no wild bears to watch out for—this time. There were other obstacles. It was easy to trip and break an ankle in this environment. They needed all hands for the fight. Bako Simovic wasn't going to go down easily.

Presently they reached the perimeter and Raven and Elena broke off to take a closer look. They found a rise near the south fence and stayed low while examining the spread. Hasanaj took his men and directed them to their positions for the opening of the attack.

A few guards roamed. One smoked a cigarette. He was easy to see when the tip of his cigarette flared, and the scent carried through the air.

Elena said, "There's only a few guards and they're far apart. We can take them."

"No noise, Elena."

"But, Raven—"

"We're ghosts until the rest of the team starts."

She grunted. Raven didn't care if she wasn't happy.

His talk with her prior to their departure hadn't achieved the results he wanted. She told him she was "fine" but it was obvious she was far from "fine" no matter how forcefully she insisted.

Raven kept his eyes on the target. He counted five roaming guards, and they didn't roam much. They walked a little, stopped, walked a little more. Only the cigarette smoker remained in motion, staying close to the fence. Now Raven wished for one of the scoped rifles some members of Hasanaj's force carried. A couple of sniper shots would knock the guards out of action fast.

The wooden fence wasn't electrified and there were no mines underground—according to Hasanaj, anyway. Raven trusted the smuggler and understood why the cartel wouldn't have such countermeasures in an area traveled by civilians, but still he wondered if there were any nasty surprises waiting.

The other variable was how many defenders the ranch had. They counted the number of guards outside, but how many were inside the main house? Bako Simovic would certainly have increased his security after the attack on Vercuni's house. No question. There were ways to discover the information, to camp out and watch the ranch for a few days, but Raven didn't think they had the time. Black Ember was going to move from the distribution center to the street, and they had to hurry. Hurrying meant improvising. Improvising meant you didn't know everything you needed but you knew enough to react once the action started. Theoretically.

They had numbers on their side. Hasanaj had been right.

There had been no shortage of volunteers. At least ten more shooters were told to remain behind; there hadn't been enough room in the choppers for everybody.

Raven watched and waited and listened to Elena's breathing beside him. He scanned not only the ranch but around it as much as possible. He was looking for the one variable they'd missed, the one surprise to foul up the operation, the missing piece—

He heard the motor before Elena.

"What's that?" she asked.

"The surprise," Raven told her.

Raven keyed the wireless communication unit on his chest rig. A corresponding earpiece was in his right ear. "Raven to Kemal."

"I hear it."

"Can you see it?"

"Not yet."

Presently the two trucks, kicking up clouds of dust, came over a rise and approached the ranch's gate. Noises within the fence line—people talking, their voices carrying. Lights snapped on in the main house. No alarm, but there might as well have been. More men ran out of the main house. Raven cursed.

"Kemal? I think they found our helicopters."

———————

BAKO SIMOVIC HAD a hard time sleeping. He kept thinking *what if*—what if whoever attacked Vercuni's house came to the ranch next? He'd added more troops to his staff, sent out the truck patrols; what more could he do? He lay in bed staring at the ceiling and wondering if it was enough.

A double knock on the door, and the knob turned. He sat

up as his chief security officer came in and turned on the light. Bako squinted against the glare.

"What is it?"

"The outer patrol found two choppers about ten miles from here. We may be under attack soon."

"Are you sure?"

"They traced some of the steps. We're looking at a large group, and they were heading in this direction."

Adrenaline surged through Bako as he jumped out of bed.

"How are the men set up?" He began shedding his pajamas and traded them for street clothes.

"They're in position. We're waiting."

Bako went to the closet where he grabbed his assault rifle and a belt of magazines. He fastened the belt around his waist.

"Then I'll go wait with them."

"Shouldn't you call—"

"I'll call while I'm waiting, yes. I'm not going to hide. Not when these sons of bitches are looking for a fight. Let's give them one."

29

RAVEN SAID TO ELENA, "YOU READY?"

"Bet your *ass*," Elena said.

Raven keyed his com unit once more. "Raven to Kemal. We're going in. We'll divert their attention and let you slide up the back side."

"Copy. Be careful."

"If we don't make it, let 'em have it."

"Understood."

"Raven out." He turned to Elena, but before he said anything more, she jumped to her feet and ran over the top of the rise toward the fence. Her boots gouged the earth, kicking up small chunks of dirt.

Raven cursed and raised his night-vision goggles away from his face. The sudden plunge into darkness, except for the glow of the moon, contrasted sharply with his earlier greenish view of the area. Elena reached the fence and both hands grasped the top and she leaped over. She landed and did a tuck and roll on the other side. Raven duplicated the maneuver and landed beside her.

"Stay," he hissed, remaining in a crouch to scan for threats. They were in a patch of shadow. Bright handheld lights popped on near the structures. Nobody had made it as far as the fence yet. But they were talking and signaling and preparing for an attack. They knew their secluded area was no longer safe. If it had ever been…

Raven smelled cigarette smoke.

And heard a man taking into a radio, alerting home base to suspected movement. He told them he was going to investigate and report back.

The voice came from his right.

Raven pivoted, lining up the glowing night sights of the Uzi, which were mounted higher to accommodate the suppressor attached to the muzzle. The SMG was set to single shot; Raven eased back the trigger as the gunman's silhouette moved against his dark background. Raven couldn't see the man's face or legs, but the outline of his upper body was clear enough. He'd ditched the cigarette, but the scent lingered. Raven aimed for the man's chest and fired twice. The gunner stopped short, as if he'd run into a wall, and collapsed in the dirt. Luckily, he'd finished his transmission and his words hadn't been cut off. But when he didn't report back, the patrols would come this way. Raven and Elena had to move fast.

"Come on," he said. He started forward, toward a small shed. No lights burned within. The shed sat in the middle of the field. Raven reached the door and pulled on the knob. Locked. But it was a solid structure to hide behind.

"My side," Elena hissed. Raven looked where she faced. More gunners converged on the fence area where they'd been. They'd find the smoker's body within a minute or two. A radio crackled. The dead smoker's radio. The boss was trying to reach him.

Elena let her Uzi do the talking, the automatic weapon sending its messengers of death to the intended targets, the suppressor attached to the barrel reducing the snap-crack of the 9mm projectiles to quiet *phuts*. Two dropped from the left-to-right burst, but Elena missed one, who immediately sounded the greater alarm of intruders within the perimeter and where to look for them. Elena fired again and ended the man's speech, but it was too late. Between one unanswered call and the cutoff of another, the defense force now had no doubt as to the arrival of unwanted guests.

Raven keyed his com unit. "Anytime, Kemal."

"Stand by."

Raven looked around the corner of the shed to the main house. About forty yards between them. He could make the sprint, but now wasn't the time. And if he misjudged the timing, he'd never make it at all.

"With me," Raven said. He broke into a run and Elena kept up. They had the advantage of darkness, but it wouldn't last long.

Then the spotlights swung their way and gunners started shouting. Raven and Elena did another tuck and roll combo to avoid the incoming fire; the crackles of the automatic weapons echoed through the night.

Raven gritted his teeth. *Where the hell is Hasanaj?*

"Raven, look!"

Raven followed Elena's gaze. A rising trail of rocket fire stretched into the night sky, and then the flaming tip exploded. A signal flare. The ranch lit up like daytime, and the heavy weapons of the Hasanaj fighters blazed into action, their louder pops and bangs drowning out the rifles and submachine guns of the defense force.

"Come on!"

Raven ran hard for the main house. Elena had no trouble keeping up.

THE FLARE FADED, and the battlefield returned to near darkness. Shadows loomed ahead as a portion of the ranch defenders closed on Raven and Elena. Both opened fire, their suppressed Uzis disguising their location for the moment, the incoming gunmen scattering, and one or two falling. Elena cursed as one of her bursts went wide, but Raven caught the gunner in the midsection with his own volley. Grabbing a grenade from his web vest, he tossed it, the resulting explosion maiming one gunner and forcing the others to run straight into the blaze of Hasanaj's attack force.

A voice in Raven's ear. "On your left!"

Raven slapped a new mag into the Uzi and turned to see Aram and Lilit running toward them. Aram said, "Can't leave you by yourself."

"Main house," Raven said. "Move out."

The three men started moving. Elena finished her reload and caught up. A cartel shooter leaned out from behind another shed, his AK-47 tracking them. Elena sprayed a burst at him, tearing a chunk of wood from the corner of the shed. Aram finished him off, the shot from his assault rifle snapping back the gunner's head. The gunner collapsed like a marionette with cut strings. Raven stayed in the lead, running hard, his heart pounding as his mind raced to keep his plan organized. He fired as he ran, not caring about hits.

The team reached the porch. Front door, a deck extending from under the front window to go around the side. Muzzles poked out the front window and Raven shouted a warning. They hit the ground as the automatic weapons spit flame. Aram cried out, Lilit returning fire in a left-to-right sweep. Lilit's salvo shattered the glass and sent pieces raining down on the shooters hiding within. Raven yelled for them to get while he fired into the house. Lilit grabbed Aram and dragged him away; Elena covered both, her Uzi bucking against her shoulder. Raven rolled right, jumped up and ran after them, tossing a grenade onto the deck. He heard the explosion and felt the shockwave but didn't see the result. He was focused on joining the others on the side of the house where there was a solid wall and no windows.

Aram sat against the wall, bleeding from an upper chest wound, Lilit working with a medical pack, and Raven and Elena standing by with their Uzis. The fighting raged around them, some of it close enough for hand-to-hand fighting, but the heavy weapons of Hasanaj and his men continued their hammering against the lighter assault weapons of the cartel force.

"Go!" Aram said, pushing Lilit away as he clutched the reddening bandage to his chest. "I'll make it. Or I won't. Go!"

"Is there a back door?" Raven asked.

"Let's find out," Lilit said.

"Keep the pressure on," Raven told Aram. "We'll be back." Then he, Elena, and Lilit ran to the rear of the house. The deck continued around to the end corner, but there was only a concrete step in front of the back door. The rear of the house faced open field, the perimeter fence, and rolling hills beyond. Raven blasted the lock on the door, kicked it open, and got out of the way as Lilit tossed a grenade inside. Elena threw another, bouncing it off a wall to go deeper into the house. They ran to get clear of the detonation, the two blasts flashing within the dark interior, a cloud of smoke drifting out the back door.

Raven ran, cutting left as he entered, firing as targets presented themselves. The kitchen table ahead was wrecked, smashed into chunks of wood, and a blown-out wall marked where the second grenade exploded. Elena and Lilit joined him. From a left hall came a pair of shooters Raven took down with a long burst; another gunner hiding behind the kitchen island felt o Elena's 9mm salvo. Lilit's assault rifle hammered at a gunner hiding behind a corner chair. They heard shouting from the rest of the house; there were more to deal with, and Bako Simovic, Raven hoped, was among them. He slapped a new mag into his Uzi and went to the entrance of the hall where the two bodies lay. He rolled a grenade along the hardwood floor and ducked back. The blast shook the house, but nobody screamed.

Hasanaj's voice buzzed in Raven's ear. "Hostiles falling back. Where are you?"

"Main house," Raven replied. He was looking into the dark hallway and hesitating. What did they face at the other end? It was a question the enemy was asking, too.

"What are you waiting for, Raven?"

He caught Elena's glare. She'd go without him if he didn't make up his mind. Why was he waiting? He looked into the dark again.

"On me," he said. Stepping over the bodies, Raven advanced with Elena and Lilit behind him. Raven moved slow and took careful steps. Elena and Lilit broke off to clear side rooms; Raven crouched and waited, then rose and resumed when they came out with all clear.

Lilit flashed a light for a second, then switched off. A right turn ahead, with a low glow showing on the facing wall. Raven moved to the corner, plucked another grenade, and tossed. He bounced it off the wall and heard it slide down the length. Men shouted. The grenade blew. Raven turned the corner at speed, his Uzi up and tracking. He entered a wide living room, the walls lined with hunting trophies—elk heads, bear pelt. Two gunners waited behind an overturned couch. Elena, beside Raven, opened fire, shooting through the couch to catch the gunners before they started shooting. Raven fired across the room, tagging another shooter hiding near a set of stairs. Lilit fired twice before another shooter brought him down; Raven pivoted to stitch the gunner chest-to-face in return. Movement from the stairs made him dive for cover. He landed in front of the overturned couch. Elena fired as she ran for a table.

The shooters in the stairwell shredded the couch, scooting back to avoid the projectiles. He swung the Uzi over the top of the couch, holding it with one hand, and loosed a spray of rounds. Elena fired and her shots shredded the wooden handrail, a few rounds nicking one of the gunners. He fell back with a yell but fired from the carpeted landing. Raven crawled around the couch, finding a table to further shield him. The gunners in the stairwell didn't notice as Elena kept them busy.

Straight ahead was a closed oak door. A line of light showed below the door, with shuffling feet interrupting the line.

Raven used his last grenade and threw it into the stairs. The two gunners hiding there had no chance. The blast sent parts of them flying across the room. Raven fired through the oak door, the 9mm slugs smacking through, leaving neat holes behind. When the door swung open, a gunner tried to toss a grenade of his own. Raven shot him in the chest. He fell back into the room, dropping the grenade. The blast picked his body off the floor and gravity sucked it back down. Raven slung the Uzi and went for his Nighthawk .45. He didn't see where Elena was; he didn't care. Bako Simovic was in the room ahead, and he closed in on the doorway with the .45 in a two-hand grip. Stepping to the right, he aimed into the room. Bed, furniture—slight movement. Two blasts from the .45 didn't bring a response.

Raven ducked low and went through the doorway. A burst of fire racked the wall to his left. He hit the floor, rolled, and cleared the corner of the bed. Bako Simovic squatted behind his desk. Part of one leg was visible under the desk. Raven shot him in the knee. Simovic screamed and fell. Raven rushed him, kicking the rifle out of his hands. The weapon slammed against the wall and Raven smacked Simovic in the side of the head with his pistol. The blow left Simovic stunned but still conscious. Raven grabbed his good leg and dragged him away from the desk to the center of the floor.

The cartel operative's squeaks and stifled groans of pain didn't register with Raven. He jammed a knee into Simovic's crotch and stuck the hot barrel of the .45 in his neck.

"Black Ember. Where?"

Simovic struggled beneath Raven but had no power to overcome the avenger's weight.

"Where's the distribution point?" Raven pressed the barrel harder into the other man's neck.

"Petra—"

"She's next. Where?"

Simovic breathed hard but forced the words out. "A warehouse—heavy guard…"

He gave the location and Raven filed it away. Elena entered the room, her Uzi held low. Raven looked at her. She shook her head. Lilit didn't make it.

Raven stood and extended his pistol. Simovic blinked, said, "No!"

"Who's the man in charge?"

"What?"

"The new boss. Who?"

"Who do you think?" Simovic found the strength to put venom behind the words. His face twisted in rage. "You have no idea who you're up against."

"Tell me."

"You know his name. General Dragoslav Mikolic. The Wolf!"

Raven's finger tightened on the trigger of the .45.

"No!"

Raven shot Simovic through the head. His body jerked once, then lay still. Simovic's eyes remained open, and Raven stared into the blank expression for a moment.

One for Irina, one for Lilit; the scales would never balance, but Raven had no intention of stopping.

He pushed past Elena to go find Lilit's body.

ELENA REMAINED in the bedroom doorway, her face a mix of shock and fear. Simovic confirmed what Ana suspected. *The Wolf*. The man who murdered her family.

As she stared at the dead man, the shock faded; fear turned to resolve. She'd finally have her chance to kill the man who destroyed her life. And if she had the opportunity, she wouldn't end his life with only one bullet.

She turned to find Raven. He kneeled beside Lilit's body. Slinging his Uzi, he picked the man up and carried him out of the room. She followed, her lips a flat line, her face almost stone-like. She had only one mission now, and she wasn't going to let Raven, Ana, or Hasanaj get in her way.

THE FIGHT OUTSIDE HAD CEASED. Hasanaj and his men stacked the dead cartel gunners and treated their wounded men. Raven set Lilit's body in front of the porch and went around the side to find Aram. The wounded man was still alert and conscious, so a medic tended to him. Raven turned away to find Hasanaj. He'd talk to Aram later.

Hasanaj found him first.

"Did you get what you needed?"

Raven nodded. "It's The Wolf."

Hasanaj nodded. "All right." He looked like he had more to say but couldn't find the words.

Raven said, "We'll finish here and keep turning up the heat. By the time we're done nobody will remember the Balkan Cartel existed."

30

Bako Simovic had provided the information about the Black Ember shipment, but he didn't say how long they had till the shipment left Montenegro. Kemal Hasanaj sent operatives to the coastal city of Bar, where the drug was being shipped, to recon the warehouse location provided by Simovic. Raven and Elena and Hasanaj made the one-hour trip within forty-eight hours, when the scouts reported activity at the warehouse. A ship had docked, crews had arrived, and the VIPs on Raven's hit list also showed up. Petra Carapic and Savan Kalezic. The recon team reported heavy security, which Raven expected. By the time the cartel heard what happened to Simovic and the ranch, they wouldn't cross the street without an armed escort.

Raven and Elena slipped through a hole they cut in the perimeter fence and crossed the warehouse back lot. Raven wasn't worried about noise. The constant racket coming from the back of the warehouse and the ship at the dock more than covered them; as always, a patrol was their biggest threat. The air was thick with salt, diesel fumes, and the faint rot of forgotten cargo, exemplified by the cast-off containers and crates spread about the back lot.

The warehouse squatted by the dock's edge, the corrugated walls scarred by rust. It didn't look like the spot for a major cartel operation. Raven crouched behind a stack of moldy crates, his Uzi gripped tightly, the weight of the SMG a familiar comfort. The rest of his combat rig felt heavy and tight on his frame, but it held other tools of his lethal trade.

The distant rumble of the ship's idling engine left no room for nighttime silence. But it was also a reminder of how fast they needed to strike. The containers being lifted onto the deck of the ship, via crane, contained the Black Ember opioids they were there to stop. The ship was Kemal Hasanaj's responsibility, and Raven wished him luck.

Elena, further away from Raven but also behind cover, whispered in his left hear through their wireless com unit.

"Two guards, coming close."

"Copy."

"They look half asleep. *Amateurs.*"

"Don't bet on it, Elena," Raven replied. The mission remained simple. Infiltrate the warehouse, destroy Black Ember, and eliminate Petra Carapic and Savan Kalezic. With his core people gone, Anton Vercuni would have no choice but to run to the big boss for help, and Raven and Elena intended to follow him into The Wolf's lair for the final showdown. Black Ember, the cartel's synthetic opioid, was no ordinary drug. It was a weapon—addictive enough to enslave cities, lucrative enough to bankroll a mercenary army aimed at seizing Serbia and turning it into The Wolf's criminal paradise. No. Raven was going to stop them even if he died trying.

Kemal Hasanaj had the task of dealing with the ship and then picking up Raven and Elena—if they made it through the fight. Despite Ana Gray's warnings of his potential duplicity, Raven had yet to see any evidence. Hasanaj appeared to be exactly what he claimed, an asset of Ana's, albeit a criminal, who wanted to even the score for Irina Vukovic's death. And he wasn't the only one.

The two guards, despite their lack of alertness, seemed capable enough to Raven. He watched them pass. They wore slung rifles. At such a late hour, a display of weapons went as unnoticed as the warehouse did during daylight hours. Raven signaled Elena with a whispered, "Go," and they moved through the maze of crates and rusted containers littering the lot. The warehouse's exterior was a fortress of neglect, but it was good camouflage for the cartel. Nobody paid any attention. Raven's pulse was steady, but his mind raced. The stakes felt heavier this time. If they killed the cartel operatives but failed to stop the ship, none of their efforts mattered.

They reached a side door, its lock spotted with rust. Elena kneeled in front of the door and went to work with her picks. Raven, his back to her, watched their six. Elena's fingers moved with surgical precision, and the lock wasn't stubborn. The tumblers clicked softly, the door groaned open, and they slipped inside. The darkness within swallowed them.

THE WAREHOUSE REEKED OF CHEMICALS, a nauseating blend of acetone and something excessively sweet—Black Ember's signature, according to Ana Gray. Flickering fluorescent lights cash harsh shadows across the concrete floor, revealing stacks of crates stamped with a black flame insignia. Forklifts and conveyor belts stood dormant. At the far end, a loading bay opened to the docks, where the cargo ship idled, its deck crawling with workers and heavy with containers. The derrick operator lifting the containers onto the deck placed the last one in position, then swung his crane away. Sweat trickled down Raven's neck. They were running out of time faster than he'd anticipated. If the ship was fully loaded, it wouldn't be long before they took to sea.

Beside him, Elena hissed, "Up there." She pointed to a raised metal platform overlooking the floor. Petra Carapic stood barking orders in Serbian, face stern, her long hair pulled into a severe bun. She wore high boots and a long skirt and sweater combo. Naughty librarian? Hardly. She was the librarian who liked hitting boys and girls with a ruler.

Beside her, Savan Kalezic, the third member of Anton Vercuni's unholy trinity, checked a tablet, his nervous energy in stark contrast to Petra's control. Four guards flanked them, armed with compact submachine guns, but they weren't the target of her tirade. She spoke to a lone man, who didn't bother to reply. Raven couldn't tell if he was part of the ship's crew or the warehouse crew, but she wasn't letting up. Somebody had screwed up somewhere, and maybe it was enough to delay the ship.

Raven studied the area around him and counted eight more guards, their movements sluggish, their attention on matters other than security. They were all chatting, passing the time, unconcerned when such a large force was present. Crates and machinery; narrow catwalks gave them the high ground if they needed it. But the open loading bay was the death trap to avoid.

"We take the guards first," Raven said. "Silent. Then the rest."

Elena nodded, her face a mask of resolve. He'd expected her to be more upset at the revelation of The Wolf truly being in charge of the Balkan Cartel, but she'd instead gone quiet, internalizing any reaction; Raven wasn't sure if she'd explode later, or keep it under control. Right now, it wasn't his concern. They split up, Raven moving left toward a cluster of crates. Elena circled right toward a row of steel drums. His boots were silent on the concrete, his breath shallow. He'd attended this dance many times, but the adrenaline never dulled.

He reached the first guard, a stock man fumbling for a cigarette. Raven's arm snaked around his neck, his combat knife slicing cleanly across the man's throat. The guard gurgled, collapsing, and Raven dragged him behind a crate, wiping the bloody blade on the man's uniform.

Across the warehouse, Elena killed another guard with her silenced Glock handgun, the double-tap of 9mm slugs sending the guard to the floor. She dragged the body out of sight.

Two down...

They moved like specters, carving through the cartel's defenses. Raven took out a third guard with a suppressed headshot, the Nighthawk .45 performing its role to perfection. The man's body crumpled silently. Elena garroted a fourth, her wire biting deep as she lowered the corpse behind a crate. But the next pair Raven encountered shattered their silent war. With his back to a side door as he waited for his next target, he spun when the door opened. Framed there were the two guards Elena spotted outside, the "amateurs," who ceased their conversation and swung up their weapons while shouting an alarm. "Intruder! Lower level!"

Raven spun around with the night sights of the .45 lining up; two shots, a shift in aim, another pair; the .45 ACP hollow-points cut the guards down. One let off a burst from his weapon as he fell back through the doorway. The rounds parked off the high ceiling. The other didn't get a chance to fire as he fell in front of the door and blocked the gap.

The warehouse exploded into chaos. The remaining

guards scrambled, and lights popped on. Petra's voice cut through from the top level. "Find them! Kill them!"

Raven dove behind a crate as bullets tore through the air, splintering wood and sparking off metal. Raven thought if they weren't careful, they'd kill each other with ricochets. Elena slid to cover beside him, then quickly rose to stitch a gunner's chest with a salvo from the Uzi. Back down and reloading as the guard's body fell, she quipped, "So much for stealth," and gave Raven a grim smile.

"Plan B," he said.

"Which is?"

"Wing it."

Raven was up, firing, driving a gunman back into hiding, Elena sending her own messengers of death at available targets. Raven and Elena exploited the crowded warehouse for everything it was worth, popping up and around like rabbits, firing precise shots. Two more guards fell, their submachine guns clattering, their comrades calling out to each other in an attempt to coordinate their response. Elena flanked Raven, walking backward. Her Uzi dropped another with a single headshot. Raven grabbed her and pulled her to the floor as a line of slugs smacked into the wood around them. He covered his face, Elena covering her eyes, then they rolled away from each other and Raven stitched a trio of rounds into the approaching gunner's chest. A fast reload and he was back on his feet.

Rapid movement caught his attention and he pivoted to face the new threat but froze on the trigger. Savan Kalezic was running, fast, dodging the obstacles, heading for a side exit. He said to Elena, "Get the woman," and ran after him.

Kalezic wasn't carrying a weapon or anything else, and he was running so hard he didn't see Raven step into the open and fire a single shot. The cartel operative's left knee popped like an egg, and he hit the ground, sliding, his skin scraping on the concrete and his scream filling the space. Raven ran to him. He was trying to crawl now, leaving a trail of red, but the pain from his shot-out knee was taking the fight out of him fast. Raven kicked him in the belly, then bent to shove Kalezic onto his back. He slung the Uzi, took out his pistol, and kneeled beside the wheezing man.

"Sucks, don't it?"

Pain was etched across Kalezic's face; his color was gone. "Who are you?"

"Get out your phone."

"What?"

"Give me your phone."

Kalezic nodded and winced as he moved, going for the outside pocket of his jacket. He gave up with a frustrated exhale. Raven reached into the pocket and grabbed the phone. It wasn't password protected, and he found the camera feature. Snapping a shot of Kalezic's twisted expression and bloody body, he found Anton Vercuni's phone number and sent him the picture. Kalezic looked at him with fear and confusion. Raven only grinned and set the phone down.

"You can't stop this," Kalezic said. "The shipment is already moving."

Raven glanced toward the dock. Sure enough, the container ship was inching away from the dock.

He stood, looked down at the man on the floor, and shook his head.

"If you only knew."

Then Raven shot the other man through the head.

Across the warehouse, Elena ran for a flight of steps leading to the catwalks and top level. She was fast, dodging between stacks. A gunner appeared from hiding, firing at her. She dropped him with a single shot. A second gunner came from her right, colliding with her in a hard tackle. They both hit the ground hard, Elena losing her grip on the Uzi. As the SMG slid across the floor, the guard adjusted his position to get his own submachine gun between them. Elena's Glock barked in response. She held the gun low against her belly, muzzle forward, and put the rounds through the gunner's abdomen. His eyes widened and a choked cry escaped his lips. Elena shoved him away and fired another shot through his head.

On her feet, pistol holstered, Uzi back in hand, she continued. Reaching the steps, she ran up the flight with Petra Carapic firing a pistol at her. But Petra couldn't aim for crap, and the shots smacked into the wall beside Elena and over her head. She ran with her head down and shoulders hunched, however—she wasn't charging headlong. When she reached the landing, Petra was out of bullets. The woman threw the gun, and Petra batted it away. The woman screamed and turned to run. Where she was heading along the narrow catwalk, Elena didn't know. What she wanted to accomplish by running was also a mystery. She had nowhere to go but a small office at the end of the catwalk, and unless she had a machine gun hidden in there with which to continue the fight, Elena saw the move as a desperate attempt leading only to doom. Elena shouldered the Uzi, aimed at the woman's back, and let her have it. The Uzi stuttered, Petra's back opened, gushing bits of red flesh like a flower petal spreading in the summer, and then she was falling, momentum still carrying her forward, and then she landed on her face. The catwalk let out a clang as it took the brunt of Petra's weight, and Petra's face acted like a brake. Her body stopped moving forward; ceased functioning altogether. Elena calmly changed magazines and snapped back the Uzi's bolt. *Always be ready*, her mentors had told her. She turned and descended the steps at a much slower pace than before.

Gunfire from the dock made her stop and drop. She peeked over the top of a crate. The ship was departing, slowly; the dock crew blocked access to the outside area, and they held automatic rifles. They were firing at Raven! She ran hard, calling his name. She didn't want him to think she was a hostile and shoot her by mistake. Stray rounds smacked into crates around her. She heard the bullets whistle; felt the smack of splinters against her exposed skin.

Raven stretched flat on the ground, crawling from crate to crate, forklift to storage barrel. He wanted to get within grenade range. The ship still loomed large but was almost clear of the dock. If Hasanaj hadn't come through…

More gunfire behind him, a sustained burst, the dock defenders falling back but unscathed. Raven looked over his shoulder at Elena as she ran to him, getting on the floor beside him.

"Keep it going!" he yelled.

She raised herself high enough to keep shooting, switching to short bursts. Raven plucked a grenade from his web vest, pulled the pin, and threw high and over. Elena ducked. The explosion rocked the warehouse, flame and debris flying toward the ceiling. The blast caught two of the shooters. Two remained. Raven yelled, "Now!" and he and Elena rose to fire and the last two shooters joined the other corpses littered around them.

They ran through the maze once more to reach the dock and watched the ship get further away. Somebody on the rear deck looked back at them and waved.

"This is not good," Elena said.

The breeze off the water cooled the sweat on Raven's skin, but his rapid pulse rate didn't abate. There was no way to stop the ship if Hasanaj had failed. Raven turned his head left, right, searching the water for Hasanaj, any sign their smuggler ally survived to accomplish his part of the mission.

A winkling flashlight—two flashes, a pause, two more—at the end of the dock spurred Raven to action once more. He grabbed Elena's arm and they started running. There was no enemy resistance left to stop them. They reached the edge of the pier and found Hasanaj in his speedboat where he was supposed to be.

"Let's go! Getting late!" he yelled.

Raven and Elena landed heavily in the smaller craft, Raven shouting, "The ship's moving, Kemal."

"Did you doubt me, my friend?" Hasanaj produced a small black box from his large jacket. It was a little smaller than a pack of cigarettes and had two buttons on it. He tossed the box to Raven. "Do the honors."

The buttons were red and green. Raven pressed the red button and turned his attention to the ship. There was a *whump* from under the waterline, then a bigger blast ruptured the exterior hull. Orange flame leaped into the night. An on-board alarm blared. Activity on the deck began a rush of running bodies. Raven grinned and tossed the detonator back to Hasanaj.

"I never doubted you for a second."

Elena, behind Raven, approached the two men. She gave Raven a nudge to get him out of the way and said to the smuggler, "Can we get out of here please?"

"Do what the lady says," Raven told the smuggler. Kemal Hasanaj dropped behind the wheel, fed the engine a little throttle, and spun the speedboat away from the dock and took off across the smooth water in the opposite direction of the sinking ship.

31

ELENA LAY AWAKE LISTENING TO RAVEN AND HASANAJ continue their conversation. Their muted voices were difficult to interpret, but she heard a few of the words through the walls. They were strategizing. Plotting next steps. Raven wanted a surveillance team on Anton Vercuni and his wife to watch them give an alert when they departed so, assuming they were going to The Wolf, the rest of Hasanaj's force, along with Raven and Elena, could follow them. Ridiculous. Too much talking. Elena had her answers and Ana Gray knew the truth and it was time to do more than only talk.

She waited in the dark bedroom until the talking ceased and waited longer for both men to fall into deep sleep. The safehouse was still foreign, still felt like an antiseptic hotel, a place for staying, not living, but she rose and dressed and found her way to the kitchen and the place on the counter where they kept the keys to the car. The only car Hasanaj had at the house. Once they discovered she was gone, Raven and Hasanaj would have to first get alternate transportation. The thought made her pause. Was a solo play really what she wanted to do?

She had a score to settle, and she wanted the accounts balanced.

So, yeah.

Her combat suit wasn't the most pleasant-smelling garment but she pulled it back on, loaded her kit bag, and left the house. *Quietly.* She knew Raven wasn't a light sleeper, but she had no idea if Hasanaj would awake at the slightest noise. The outside chill and crickets greeted her. The black Mercedes sat in the driveway, and a press of the key fob opened the locks. The headlamps flashed, too, highlighting the garage door; she didn't think anybody inside would see the flare. Getting into the car, she started the engine, backed out, and drove away. She knew where to go. There was no need to consult a map. She had the route memorized. Burned into her brain, even. She'd know how to get to Anton Vercuni's house blindfolded, if necessary.

Time to settle a score.

Elena drove with a grim set to her face and murder on her mind.

HE TOLD his wife he was working late.

Lieutenant Vojin Stojanovic hated lying to her, but didn't see any other way to get the freedom he needed for what he wanted to do. When she asked when he'd be home, he told her he didn't know—which was true, very true—but also not to wait up. Part of him wondered if he was coming back.

With the destruction of major Balkan Cartel facilities in the last forty-eight hours, pressure from Anton Vercuni was at its peak. He was asking for too much, especially with the department watching him, albeit quietly; he knew they were in the background wherever he went. Phantoms, chasing him. Vercuni wanted information on the "strike force"—and he didn't want to hear Stojanovic say he knew nothing. The police *had* to know something, and Stojanovic was hiding critical information. Well, in a perfect world, they would, but Stojanovic had to admit he was as stumped as anybody else on the "official" side of law enforcement. Somebody was hitting the cartel, all right, and hitting them where it counted. He wondered if the activity was somehow connected to Irina Vukovic, and, if so, he wished the fighters Godspeed. They were doing more to avenge her death than he was able to.

Stojanovic was desperate for a way out, and the only way was to stack some bodies of his own. Whoever hit the cartel knew what they were doing. He hoped with Vercuni dead and one of his major distributors dead too, he could clear out any evidence pointing to him, anybody who knew what he'd done, and save his career. And his life. Tall order? Probably. But he had to try or die. There was no other way.

He drove a city car because he wanted some mark of official duty. He drove with the radio off. Traffic was light. He didn't speed. First stop, Colonel Kovac's nightclub. He hoped Kovac was still there. He planned to leave Kovac there if he found him. Otherwise, he'd proceed to his second target.

Anton and Melika Vercuni. He knew where they lived, too.

ELENA HAD no intention of driving up the curving access road to the Vercuni house. She was already having flashbacks to the night she drove to the house the first time, when they caught her peeking through a computer she found in an office; the chill she felt wasn't from the cold air coming in through the open windows. She'd rolled them down to dry the sweat on her skin, but nothing calmed her racing heart.

She was going back into the lion's den, alone, and questioning ever leaving the safehouse. But it was too late to go back. It was now or never.

She parked the Mercedes off the road and grabbed her kit bag from the passenger seat. Taking out the Uzi (she hadn't had a chance to clean it since the action at the dock), her web gear, and assorted accessories, she donned the gear and started up the sloping hill to the house. Security lights burned on the outer perimeter, lighting up part of the house. She knew about the sentries. They wouldn't be too hard to take down. Elena only hoped there weren't too many.

Crouched in the shadow on the slope, she watched the portion of the outer wall visible from her vantage point; she watched for gunners patrolling the outside. None came across. They'd all be on the other side of the wall and inside the house.

Her mouth was dry and her hands shook. But she tightened her grip on the Uzi, took a deep breath, and continued her climb toward the wall. She wasn't sure where her infiltration point would be yet, but she'd find it within minutes. Several, very fast minutes.

32

SHE CLIMBED HIGHER AND STOPPED TO LISTEN; STILL NO SIGN she'd been detected. Her boots sank into the soft dirt with each step. Elena tried to remember if they had any sensors in the ground but then realized her first visit had not covered such a topic. She'd been there on the auspices of selling guns to the cartel after the sudden "retirement"—the lethal kind, thanks to another of Ana Gray's operatives—of their previous supplier. They hadn't talked about the security around the house. She'd arrived by car, for heaven's sake; totally different mode of entry than she attempted now. Elena climbed the slope, going faster, finally reached the wall. Her legs felt the strain of the climb but hadn't turned to jelly. What she now wanted was a ladder to help get over the top. What she had in her back would have to suffice.

She slid the pack off her back and extracted the grappling hook and nylon rope. It wasn't a hard toss. The hook locked onto the top of the wall, and she climbed up the side, pausing to peek over the top, then rolling over to land opposite in a low crouch. Gripping the Uzi with both hands, she scanned for targets while trying to check her surroundings at the same time. Melika's garden, by the look of the patch of dirt she'd landed in; roses, tomato plants, and other vegetables grew around her. Marble statues were mixed within the rows and helped conceal her from the prying eyes about ten yards away. A pair of guards stopped talking to look in the direction of the garden. They casually cradled their submachine guns but took firmer grips on the weapons as they started in her direction. One spoke into a radio.

Elena cursed and looked for a way out. To her left, the garden continued along the wall but eventually ended at grass. To the right, the patio lead to the back of the house.

The approaching guards started moving faster. Two more came around the corner, on the far side of the house. They knew she was there. Elena chose the only option available. Attack first.

Uzi to her shoulder, she took out the nearest threat: the guards approaching from the front. The Uzi chattered in full auto. One guard dropped, the other tried diving for the grass, but Elena tracked his roll and fired again, pinning him to the grass with the three-round burst. She pivoted, rising slightly, and triggered another salvo at the guards coming from the house. They rolled behind patio furniture; she couldn't get a sight picture. But they zeroed in on her. She ran as they fired single shots. As she ran into the open, heading for the far end of the yard, she fired at the house. Tripping on a crack in the cement and tumbling, she managed to recover and stop on her belly. The bullets aimed at her split the air overhead. She fired back, missing, and hurried to reload. Aiming toward the patio once more, she found no targets. The two gunners were well-concealed. Her eyes darted back and forth as she searched. Where had they gone? The crackles of gunfire began to fade, but the ringing in her ears did not. She hurried to move back toward the shadows of the far yard, and the wall there; maybe a quick hop over and back to the car was the best option. If she stayed in the fight, she wasn't going to get out alive.

Elena scrambled toward the shadowed edge of the yard, her breath ragged, the Uzi slick in her sweating palms. The wall loomed ahead, her only shot at escape, but the silence behind her felt wrong—too heavy, too deliberate. She risked a glance back. The patio was empty, the furniture still, but a faint rustle came from the garden to her left. Her heart sank. They were flanking her.

She broke into a sprint, the wall now just yards away, but a sharp crack split the air—a sniper's round, not from the house but from above. The bullet grazed her calf, a hot sear of pain, and she stumbled, crashing into the dirt. The Uzi skittered from her grip, landing just out of reach. She lunged for it, but boots crunched closer, too many, too fast. A shadow loomed over her, and the cold steel of a blade pressed against the back of her neck.

"Welcome back, Elena," a low voice growled. *Anton Vercuni's voice!*

Elena froze, her mind racing for an out, but the numbers were against her. Four guards materialized from the darkness, guns trained on her. The sniper's laser dot danced on her chest, a fifth threat pinning her in place. She'd miscalculated, underestimated their response time, their coordination. *No. That's not what you did. You went off half-cocked because you let emotion get in the way of good sense. Just like last time.*

The cartel wasn't just muscle; they were disciplined.

Rough hands yanked her arms behind her back, a zip tie biting into her wrists. The same rough hands rolled her onto her back. Two men stood above her. One was the hulk named Dede Bizi. The other was Anton Vercuni, and he held a knife. He gave Bizi a nudge, and the big man moved away. Vercuni kneeled beside her, his face half-lit by the glow of the house. Her eyes were wide, her breathing shallow. He smirked and ran the flat side of the knife across her lips.

"We're going to pick up where we left off, young lady."

He brushed the razor edge against her cheek. She stopped breathing. Stopped moving.

"You're going to talk this time."

He gave the order and the guards hauled her to her feet, her injured leg screaming as she staggered. The Uzi lay abandoned in the dirt, her pack still tangled in the garden. No weapons, no backup, no way out. Elena's eyes flicked to the wall one last time, so close yet impossibly far, as they dragged her toward the house. The cartel's boss would want answers—answers she didn't have. She'd bitten off more than she could chew, and now they'd make her choke on it.

33

THE BASEMENT REEKED OF DAMP CONCRETE. ELENA SAT BOUND to a metal chair, her wrists and ankles secured with zip ties cutting into her skin. The single bulb overhead cast harsh shadows, illuminating Anton Vercuni as he paced before her, his custom Damascus steel knife glinting in his hand. Its serrated edge caught the light, a wicked promise of pain. Elena's heart pounded, but she forced her face into a mask of defiance, her jaw clenched tight.

She fought the flashbacks while feeling the bugs across her skin...

"Who do you work for?" Anton's voice was low. He stepped closer, twirling the knife. "You're no gun runner. You and your friends are too clean, too trained. Except for this latest disaster. Coming in alone? *Why?* Who sent you? I know it isn't the CIA or MI6. Who, Elena? *Who?*"

Elena spat at his feet, her voice steady despite the ache in her bruised ribs. "You're paranoid. I'm just a freelancer who got in over her head. No one's coming for me this time."

He smirked, unconvinced, and leaned in, the knife hovering

near her throat. With a flick of his wrist, he sliced through the collar of her tactical shirt, the fabric parting like paper. The cold steel grazed her skin, not cutting but close enough to make her breath hitch. "Talk, or I carve you into something less pretty."

She glared, her mind racing for leverage, but the ties held firm, and her weapons were long gone. "You're wasting your time," she hissed. "I work alone."

Anton's smile vanished. He slashed again, cutting away a sleeve, the knife's edge whispering against her arm. "Who is Ana Gray?" he said, his voice hardening.

Elena stayed stoic.

"Who is Ana Gray, Elena?"

"Never met her."

"Really? Irina Vukovic knew her. I saw the emails on her computer. My wife found them. Are you one of Ana Gray's operatives, Elena? Tell me about her network. Tell me where I can find her."

Elena's stomach twisted, but she forced a laugh, brittle and sharp. "You think I'm part of some grand conspiracy? I'm a hired gun, you idiot. Keep cutting, you'll get nothing but blood."

He grabbed her chin, forcing her to meet his gaze, the knife now at her collarbone. "I don't believe you." Another slash, and her shirt hung in tatters, exposing her to the chill of the basement. Her skin prickled, but she refused to flinch, staring him down even as her pulse thundered.

"Anton!" A sharp voice cut through the tension. Melika stood at the basement door, her silhouette framed by the dim light from the stairs. Her tone was icy, commanding. "Enough. The Wolf wants her. Face-to-face."

Anton froze, his knife still poised. His face twisted with frustration. His grip on the knife tightened, his knuckles white. "This is the second time!" he shouted. "First, he wanted her sent to the compound, and you saw the results. Total debacle. No! This time she's mine to break!"

Melika's expression didn't waver. "Take it up with him. He's expecting us."

"We're taking her to *Serbia*?"

"Those are our orders, Anton."

With a snarl, Anton sheathed the knife and stepped back, glaring at Elena. "You're so lucky." He turned to Melika, his voice bitter. "Fine."

Elena's chest heaved as they left, her body trembling but her resolve unbroken. The Wolf. She was finally going to face him. All she had to do was stay alive long enough to put a bullet through his head, a knife through his neck, or find another deadly implement with which to achieve her vengeance. Resolve gripped her. This is what she'd been waiting for...

THE NEON GLOW of the nightclub faded in Lieutenant Vojin Stojanovic's rearview mirror as he trailed Peter Kovac's sleek black Audi through the late-night streets of Podgorica. The city hummed with a restless energy, its pulse beating along Bulevar Svetog Petra Cetinjskog, where bars and cafés spilled light onto the pavement. Stojanovic kept a steady distance in his unmarked police cruiser. His hands gripped the wheel, knuckles pale, the weight of his decision pressing against his chest. Irina Vukovic's face—young, fierce, like his daughter's—haunted him. Her blood on the cartel's hands was the final straw. He'd been their dog long enough, leashed by his wife's old medical bills. Now, he'd bite back.

Kovac's Audi veered onto Ulica Slobode, slowing as it approached the quieter stretch near the Morača River. Stojanovic flicked on his lights, a single pulse of red and blue, flashing from their dashboard mounts. The Audi pulled over, gravel crunching under its tires, just past the stone arches of the Millennium Bridge. Stojanovic parked behind, his Beretta 9mm heavy in its holster. He stepped out, the night air sharp with the river's damp chill, and approached the driver's side, his flashlight casting a stark beam.

Kovac rolled down the window, his slick hair and gold chain glinting. "Vojin, what's this about?" His voice was casual, but his eyes narrowed, calculating. "You picking me up for a late coffee?"

"Step out, Colonel Kovac," Stojanovic said, his tone flat, betraying nothing. The bridge's lights reflected off the river, a shimmering distraction, but his focus was iron.

Kovac smirked, unbuckling his seat belt. "Anton's got you working overtime, huh?" He swung the door open and stood, hands in his pockets, cocky. "What's the problem?"

Stojanovic's jaw tightened. Irina's articles had named Kovac, linked him to the cartel's smuggling routes. She'd died for it. "You're the problem," he said, voice low. "Irina Vukovic. Remember her?"

Kovac's smirk faltered, his hand twitching toward his jacket. Stojanovic was faster. The Beretta was out in a heart-beat, and before Kovac could speak, Stojanovic fired—a single shot through the forehead. Kovac crumpled, blood pooling on the asphalt, his gold chain glinting dully. Stojanovic scanned the empty street, pulse steady, then dragged the body to the riverbank and shoved it into the Morača's dark current. The water swallowed Kovac without a sound.

Back in the cruiser, Stojanovic's hands shook, but his resolve held. Next was Anton Vercuni. He pulled onto Cetinjski Put, heading north out of Podgorica. The city's lights gave way to the shadowed slopes of the Kuči Moun-tains, where Vercuni's mountaintop villa crouched like a predator overlooking the valley. The road twisted past the skeletal ruins of Doclea, ancient stones stark against the night, and climbed toward Tološi. Stojanovic's mind churned. Vercuni and Melika would be home, maybe with guards, maybe with Elena, that woman they'd caught. He didn't care. He'd kill them all if it meant breaking free. The cruiser's engine growled as he accelerated, the villa's distant lights winking through the pines. Time to end this.

34

ANTON VERCUNI RETURNED HIS KNIFE TO THE COLLECTOR'S case and turned to face Dede Bizi. The big man stood near the door.

"I need you to come with us," Vercuni said.

"Of course."

"You know. Just in case."

Bizi nodded. He'd been quiet in the days following the shootout at the hotel where he, his hired guns, and Colonel Kovac had gone to try and find the commando and the spy—Elena Covaci. He could use her name now.

"The Wolf is upset with us," Vercuni said. "The Black Ember is gone. Associates are dead." He pressed his lips together. "How am I going to explain it all, Dede?"

"You have the woman."

"Can The Wolf make her talk when I couldn't?"

"He won't have another woman running interference."

Vercuni frowned. "You mean Melika—"

"It's as cold as you or me."

"You have a point."

"And she won't sit around and let a woman be tortured in her house."

"Hmmm."

"Surprised you didn't think of it yourself, Anton."

"Yeah, well. You know me." His frown turned thoughtful. "Wait. We know about Ana Gray. We know she has something to do with this, but not how. We have the emails where she tells Irina Vukovic to start digging into the cartel. So, we bring this evidence to The Wolf, he makes Elena confirm what we think, and—"

"You're off the hook. The Wolf won't string you up."

"I wouldn't put it in so many words," Vercuni said, "but, yeah."

Vercuni smiled and laughed to himself. His ideas needed time to process. Breaking Elena himself wasn't the best idea; bringing everything to The Wolf was the *better* idea. Give the big boss the means to solve their problem. And, sure, keep The Wolf from shooting him and Melika and Dede, if he felt the urge.

"How long till the plane is ready?" he asked Bizi.

"Pilot said at least an hour for the pre-flight check and fueling."

"Good! Time to pack. Let's go."

Bizi held the door for his boss and they went out.

ELENA SAT in the dimly lit living room, her wrists bound with fresh zip ties, the plastic cutting into her bruised skin. Her tactical suit hung in tatters, courtesy of Anton's earlier knife work, and her calf throbbed where the sniper's bullet had grazed her. She kept her eyes sharp, scanning for an opening, but the odds were grim. Anton Vercuni and his wife Melika moved with cold precision, packing his-and-her duffels with essentials. Dede Bizi, their hulking henchman, loomed near the door, a submachine gun slung across his chest, eyes flicking between Elena and the windows.

"We leave in five," Melika said, her voice like a blade, cutting through the tension. She zipped the duffel and glanced at Anton. "The Wolf expects us by dawn."

Elena's mind raced. Serbia. The Wolf. The name alone sent a chill through her, but at the same time activated reserve strength. *Relax. They're taking you to the enemy. When the moment comes you can end him.* She tested the zip ties, twisting her wrists subtly, but they held fast. Her eyes darted to Dede, then to the window overlooking the gravel drive-way. The Kuči Mountains stretched beyond, their dark slopes a taunting reminder of the freedom she'd almost reached.

"Move her," Melika ordered, nodding to Dede. The henchman grabbed Elena's arm, yanking her to her feet. She stumbled, her injured leg protesting, but kept her expression defiant. Dede's grip was iron, his breath sour as he leaned close. "No tricks, or I break your neck."

"The hell you will. You *need* me."

Anger flashed across Bizi's face, but he didn't argue.

That's right, thug. You can't hurt me.

They shuffled toward the garage, Anton leading the way, Melika behind with the duffels. The villa's opulence—marble floors, gilt-framed paintings—felt like a mockery of the violence from which it was born. Outside, the night was still, the stars sharp above the pines. A black SUV idled in the driveway, its engine a low growl. Bizi shoved Elena toward the back door, but she dragged her feet, creating any chance to slow them down.

What are you hoping for?

Raven isn't coming this time.

Stop! They are taking you to The Wolf!

Anton opened the driver's side door, pausing to scan the road below. "Hurry up," he snapped. Melika slid into the passenger seat, her eyes on her phone, likely coordinating with the airport. Bizi pushed Elena into the back seat, climbing in beside her, his gun resting across his lap. The SUV's interior smelled of leather and gun oil, a fitting coffin if she didn't find a way out.

As Anton started the engine, headlights flashed across the driveway, followed by the screech of tires. An unmarked police cruiser skidded to a halt, blocking the SUV's path. Elena's pulse spiked. A cop? Here? Anton cursed, his hand going to his knife. Melika's head snapped up, her calm fracturing. "Who the hell is this?"

The cruiser's door flew open, and Lieutenant Vojin Stojanovic leaped out, his 9mm Beretta already drawn. His face was haggard, eyes burning with desperation Elena didn't understand. Blood stained his sleeve—Kovac's, she'd later learn—but his aim was steady as he advanced, the cruiser's headlights casting his shadow long and jagged.

"Anton!" Stojanovic shouted, his voice raw. "We need to talk!"

Anton stepped out of the SUV, his hand hovering near his holstered pistol. "Vojin? What's this about?" His tone was wary, suspicion creeping in.

Stojanovic's lips curled, a bitter edge to his words. "Kovac's floating in the Morača. You're next." His eyes flicked to Elena, then back to Anton. "I'm done being your dog."

Stojanovic snapped up the Beretta and he fired. Two shots, aimed at Anton's chest. But Dede Bizi was faster. From the back seat, he shoved the SUV door open. The 9mm slugs punched into the glass and deflected. Bizi unleashed a burst from his submachine gun. The rounds caught Stojanovic in the shoulder and thigh, spinning him to the ground. He hit the gravel with a cry, his Beretta clattering away, blood pooling beneath him.

"Get in!" Melika barked, slamming her hand on the dashboard. Anton jumped back into the driver's seat, flooring the gas. The SUV lurched forward, swerving around Stojanovic's cruiser, tires kicking up gravel. Bizi yanked the door shut, his gun still trained on the driveway as they sped down the winding road. Elena twisted in her seat, catching a glimpse of Stojanovic's crumpled form through the rear window. He was alive, clutching his wounds, but fading fast.

They didn't notice!

Inside the SUV, tension choked the air. Anton gripped the wheel, his knuckles white, muttering curses.

"Focus," Melika snapped.

Elena breathed deep. The airport wasn't far, and with it, Serbia and The Wolf. She needed a plan. *Fast.*

The SUV roared past the ruins of Doclea, the ancient stones a blur in the moonlight, and merged onto the E65 toward Podgorica Airport. Streetlights flashed by, softening the city's edges into industrial sprawl. Elena's heart pounded, but she kept her face blank, hiding the spark of defiance within. The Wolf might be waiting, but she wasn't done fighting.

Back in the driveway, Stojanovic lay sprawled on the gravel, blood soaking his clothes. Pain seared his shoulder and leg, each breath a knife in his chest. The night sky stretched above, stars indifferent to his struggle. His Beretta was out of reach, his strength ebbing. Irina's face flickered in his mind—her courage, her defiance, so like his daughter's. He'd failed her, failed himself. The cartel had owned him too long, and now, maybe, this was the end. He groaned, fingers clawing at the gravel, willing himself to move. But the darkness pressed in, and his eyes fluttered, the stars blurring as he wondered if he'd ever see dawn.

Gravel crunched as another car came up the drive. He raised his head to look into the blinding headlamps. The car jerked to a stop. Was this help, or more of Anton's goons coming to finish him off?

Two men climbed out of the car.

RAVEN AND HASANAJ shared the same reaction to discovering Elena's vanishing act. There was only one place she would go: straight to the Vercuni house. The problem was she took the car, and Hasanaj had to call one of his men to bring them another. When the car arrived, they left the driver to hold the fort at the safe house while they hurried to the Vercuni property and Raven hoped they weren't too late.

The speeding vehicles passing them on the way up the hill could have been anybody and no one alerted Raven's instincts. When Hasanaj turned to go through the open gate at the Vercuni house, Raven knew they were arriving well after any action. He needed to see what bodies remained.

Finding an unknown man lying in a pool of blood in the driveway was not what he had in mind. Hasanaj braked the car to a halt and the headlamps shined on the bleeding man, who shifted enough for Raven to know he wasn't dead. Out of the car, keeping the Uzi close, Raven reached the man and kneeled beside him. The badge on the man's belt told Raven all he needed to know.

"How bad are you hurt?"

"The big one had lousy aim. Left shoulder, upper chest," the man said, biting back the pain. "You're not one of them," he added.

"Neither are you. Are they gone?"

The wounded man nodded twice, sharply. He explained his arrival and what he saw before the shooting. He didn't explain why he was there, and Raven didn't ask. He was only concerned with news about "the woman."

"You're sure she wasn't hurt?"

"They had her tied."

"Is there a radio in your car?"

"Yeah, just—"

"Raven!"

Hasanaj shouted the warning as he took cover behind the door of the car. Raven saw the pair of gunners emerging from the house. He stepped in front of the cop and let the Uzi rip. The burst cut down the first of the pair and knocked him back into his partner, who took the impact of Raven's second burst and fell against the door. The door swung back against his weight, and he fell half in, half out. The other man sprawled at his partner's feet.

Raven turned and found Hasanaj helping the cop to sit up against one of his back tires. He told Raven how to use the radio to call for backup and an ambulance. Raven followed his instructions and then started for the house.

"Where you going?" Hasanaj said.

"Gotta find out where they went."

"Cops will be here fast!"

"Then we better not waste time arguing."

Hasanaj wanted to say more, but Raven was right. He watched the American step over the bodies and enter the house.

He kneeled next to the wounded man.

"What's your name?"

"Stojanovic. Lieutenant Stojanovic. Who is *that* man?"

"He's here to stop Vercuni and his boss."

"Good. Don't worry about me. I've bent the rules for the bad guys long enough. Now I'll bend them for the good guys."

"Did you know Irina Vukovic?"

Stojanovic nodded.

"So did I," Hasanaj said.

HASANAJ MADE sure not to drive too fast on the way back down the hill and stopped in a pull-out when the lights and sirens of the responding emergency crews raced by in the opposite direction.

"We made it just in time," the smuggler said.

Raven held onto a pair of laptop computers on his lap. As Hasanaj started down again, he hoped there was a clue on one of them pointing which way to go. The Vercunis had Elena. They could be anywhere. But he had a feeling they were running straight to The Wolf himself.

35

THE LAPTOPS DIDN'T ADD MUCH TO WHAT THEY DIDN'T already know, but the data Raven found added enough. An email alert sent to The Wolf from Melika Vercuni explained the capture of Elena and suspicions of her being part of a private spy network. The Wolf decided this was the prime opportunity to talk to her once more, but he wanted to handle the questioning himself, in his secure retreat, away from threats. He told Melika he'd be increasing his security force to prevent what happened in Albania from repeating.

Raven didn't have the skill set or equipment to trace The Wolf's email address in hopes of finding where the message originated from. But Ana Gray and her people did. Raven gave Ana an update over the phone and forwarded the message. She told him and Hasanaj to assemble an army of their own and get on a plane. She'd be in touch while they were in the air.

"Tell me who The Wolf is," Raven asked Hasanaj. They were driving once again, Hasanaj being the wheel, the back seat packed with gear.

"General Dragoslav Nikolic," the smuggler said. "He's Serbian."

"I wish we knew more about his retreat. Is it a fortress?"

"Probably not. If he's using a property the cartel has held for a long time, I think I know which one it is."

"And if he isn't?"

"Then what is it you say? *Punt?*"

"Wing it," Raven corrected.

THE SERBIAN MOUNTAINS loomed dark and jagged under the moonless sky. Their peaks clawed at the clouds above Zlatibor, thirty kilometers southwest of Belgrade. The sprawling villa belonging to General Dragoslav Nikolic, a.k.a. The Wolf, stuck out like the proverbial sore thumb in the valley of green. The white stone walls surrounding the property and its red-tiled roofs glowed under the glare of security lights. Reinforced glass windows glinted like a predator's eyes, and armed sentries patrolled the perimeter. The villa was a fortress, but not strong enough to withstand the incoming storm.

Facing the front of the house was an acre of green grass, the wide space enclosed only by the white walls and an iron gate. The road leading to the villa was long and sometimes treacherous from lack of maintenance, so Anton Vercuni chose another way to reach The Wolf's lair.

A white helicopter with its cabin crowded with passengers passed from the dark sky and into the glare of the security lights. The skids touched down on a landing pad in the center of the grassy field. When the pilot cut the motor, the blades spinning atop the chopper slowed to still silence, and the whisper of the night's breeze replaced the noise of the helicopter engine.

The doors opened on either side of the cabin. Anton Vercuni stepped out first, felt the chill of the wind, and wished for a heavier jacket. He turned and helped Melika out. She shivered, too. On the opposite side, Dede Bizi took solid hold of Elena Corvaci's right arm and pulled her out. The big man joined Anton and Melika.

"Nobody to meet us?" Melika asked.

"Here they come."

Anton pointed at an approached Jeep which emerged from a garage hidden from view and crossed the grassy to them.

Anton Vercuni and his party waited as a pair of icy eyes watched them from the top floor of the house.

DRAGOSLAV NIKOLIC, a.k.a. The Wolf, closed the blinds as the Jeep reached the helicopter. He'd meet them at the front door, and turned from the window to leave his den. The quiet walk along the hall to the stairs gave him a moment to think about what brought the Vercunis to his doorstep.

Nikolic was a rough-looking fifty-five. He could have passed for ten years older. Decades of hard living gave him the poor skin tone and pockmarks on his face and body, the lines, the bristly hair on his head. His eyes were dark and vivid yet no friendliness existed behind them. The only thing one saw when looking at Nikolic was a killer waiting for a silent signal to strike.

He was a former Serbian military officer who took a big part in ethnic cleansing during the Yugoslav Wars. The excuse to murder undesirables was too good to pass up, and he and his crew went overboard in their participation so much The Hague placed Nikolic on a wanted list. It was then a carefully devised "death" took Nikolic off the playing field, but he emerged as an underworld crime figure who used military connections to dominate the Balkan drug trade. When the opportunity arrived to take over the entire Balkan Cartel, he jumped at the chance. One place crash, and one dead leader, later, he was in the seat of power, and there was nobody brave enough to challenge him. Nobody brave enough to look into his icy eyes.

Nikolic descended the stairs carefully. He was a man who did not rush. Nothing was so urgent as to require speed. Slow, calculated, cold—the motto he lived by. When they opened the door and stepped out onto the well-lit porch, he had to shield his eyes from the headlamps of the Jeep. It was driving back across the grass and making a slight turn to stop before the porch. Nikolic lowered his arm as the Jeep turned so its driver's side faced him. He frowned at the hostage, the blond woman in the combat black suit. Her face wasn't familiar. Who was she, and why was she attempting to murder the Vercunis?

Anton and Melika looked well enough, and he noticed Melika carried a heavy briefcase. Her husband approached the porch but stopped halfway. All he was missing was a salute. Instead, he said, "Hello, General," with a slight bow.

"Anton."

"We brought our hostage."

"I see."

"Where would you—"

Nikolic didn't snap his fingers or give an order. Three armed men appeared from the shadows, startling Anton Vercuni. Nikolic watched them take the woman from Dede Bizi and lead her away—somewhere out of sight. Nikolic noted she was staring at him as his men took her. She didn't argue or resist. She stared at him as if fascinated. She wasn't scared. She made contact with those icy eyes and didn't flinch.

Nikolic didn't hear anything else Anton said on the porch. His mind was busy trying to remember the woman's face, because he had a feeling she knew his.

36

IT WAS HIM!

He was older, but so was she. What hadn't changed was his eyes. She'd never forget those eyes no matter how the man's face changed.

Meeting his stare was a victory in and of itself. She saw the wheels turning behind his eyes. She looked at him and didn't shrink back.

Now the hard part.

She had to withstand whatever violence he intended to dish out in order to make her talk.

But the stare.

He wouldn't forget the stare.

She had thrown him off, and he wouldn't truly get rough until he understood how she could pull off the look nobody else attempted.

Two of the armed men had her by each arm. The other walked in front of them. They led her around the villa to a narrow hallway and through a door. A set of steps led down into darkness. Elena didn't fight or argue. She took a deep breath and let them escort her down. Whatever happened next, she'd do what she had to do to survive. Because she was sure of one thing. Raven wasn't coming to rescue her this time. She was on her own.

———————————

THE BASEMENT beneath the villa was a tomb of concrete and shadow, at least in the cramped area where they deposited Elena. A light bulb hung from the ceiling, and the bright light burned hot. One of the three gunmen grabbed a folding chair from a dark corner and slammed it into the center of the room under the light. One of the other two hit Elena on the back of the head with his hand. The blow shocked her out of her stoic state, the light cry escaping her lips replaced by a louder one as the men's hands grabbed her and began pulling and slicing at the black suit and her underwear. They shoved her onto the cold metal chair and their leader was there with zip ties and straps to hold her in place. The men remained stone-faced and passive, operating like robots; when they were done, neither gave her a backward glance as they departed and left her in the cold under a hot light.

She tried to control her rapid breathing, shutting her eyes to disappear into a place of safety, but she couldn't concentrate. Because she felt the bugs again, crawling up and down her skin...

Elena did something she'd never done before when faced with such a situation.

She finally screamed. Long and loud.

———————————

THE STUDY of General Dragoslav Nikolic—The Wolf—was a sanctum of dark wood and leather, its air thick with cigar smoke. Nikolic stood by a floor-to-ceiling window, his silver hair catching the lamplight, his tailored suit immaculate despite the late hour. His eyes, cold and predatory, scanned the valley below, where the pines whispered secrets to the night. Across from him, Anton Vercuni slouched in a leather armchair, his custom Damascus steel knife spinning idly in his hand, his face a mask of barely contained frustration. Melika Vercuni sat at a mahogany desk, her fingers poised over a sleek laptop, its screen casting a pale glow on her sharp features. The laptop, so Melika claimed, held the key to their current obsession: Elena, the prisoner in their basement.

Melika's voice cut through the silence, precise and cold. "Irina Vukovic's files are a goldmine. Encrypted, but sloppy—her security was easy for me to crack."

A smile pulled at the corners of Anton's mouth. His wife didn't like it when somebody mentioned how cocky she became when discussing computer security and her ability to manipulate it like a wizard. He wasn't going to ruin her moment in the spotlight, though.

"I traced a string of emails to a server in London," Melika continued. "An address in Mayfair, 17 Grosvenor Square. Registered to a shell company, but the name behind it is Ana Gray." She leaned back, her eyes flicking to Nikolic. "The heiress. Philanthropist by day, spymaster of her own intelligence organization by night. Elena's one of hers."

Anton snorted, his knife pausing mid-spin. "A rich bitch playing spymaster. Sounds like a fantasy, but it's the word on the street, General."

Nikolic nodded. "You sure about this, Melika?"

Melika's gaze hardened, her voice like a blade. "These emails from Gray don't lie. She was telling Irina what they needed and who might help, specifically a smuggler named Hasanaj. Mean anything?"

Nikolic nodded again but didn't elaborate. He turned

from the window, his hands clasped behind his back, his presence commanding the room. "Interesting," he said quietly, his gravelly voice low, accented with the weight of his Serbian roots.

Anton sheathed his knife. "Elena's not just a lone wolf. She's got a pack behind her. I say we send a team to London. Dede Bizi can lead. Hit this Gray woman and cut the head off the snake. Problem solved."

Nikolic shook his head, his expression darkening. "Not yet. We need confirmation. If Gray's network is as deep as you say, Melika, we can't afford a misstep. A hit in London draws attention—MI6, Interpol, maybe worse." He paused, his gaze drifting toward the door, beyond which the basement stairs descended to their prisoner. "Elena's the key. She knows Gray's operation. We break her, we get the truth."

Anton smirked, cracking his knuckles. "Let me at her again. My knife was starting to get answers before you pulled me off, General. She's tough, but nobody holds out forever."

Melika's lips pressed into a thin line, her voice sharp. "We need her talking, not bleeding out."

Anton's face flushed, but he bit back a retort, glancing at Nikolic for support. The general's eyes instead were distant.

Anton stood, restless, his hand hovering near his knife. "So what? We sit here while Gray's people pick us apart? Elena's in the basement, naked, tied to a chair. She's got nothing—no backup, no tricks. Let me carve the truth out of her. I'll have her singing in an hour."

Nikolic raised a hand, silencing him. "No. I'll handle Elena myself." His lips curled into a cold smile. "I broke men in the war when you both were still children. She'll talk, or she'll die."

SHE STOPPED SCREAMING AFTER A WHILE, but her ears hurt from the sounds erupting from her lungs. Breathless, head down, waiting, Elena sat in the chair and the room's chill made her skin prickle. When the sound of the door squeaking open at the top of the steps reached her, she raised her head, defiant, and took a deep breath. Footsteps echoed on the stairs. Slow, deliberate steps. Whoever was coming to her wasn't in any hurry. And then General Dragoslav Nikolic, The Wolf, emerged into the circle of light.

She met his eyes again and he remained locked with hers. His expression was one of curiosity. If he noticed she was nude, he gave no indication. None of his guards flanked him. He was alone. She wasn't sure it gave her an advantage. His gunmen wouldn't be far away.

"Who are you?" His voice was gravelly, accented, each word precise. "Give me your name."

Elena's jaw tightened. The restraints holding her to the chair made her body ache, and her lungs hurt from scream-ing. She answered and her voice remained steady. "You don't get my name until I get answers from you."

A chuckle. "You are in no position to bargain, young lady. Why are you here? Why target *my* organization? Who sent you?" He leaned closer, hands braced on his knees, and his eyes remained on hers. He wasn't interested in her pale white nudity. "And who are your associates? The American. Give me the identity of the American, and I'll return your cloth-ing. We only needed to check it for tracking devices."

"You forgot to look in my asshole. I keep everything there."

Another chuckle, and Nikolic straightened. "You are a fighter."

Elena's pulse quickened, but she kept her face a stiff mask to hide the turmoil inside her.

"You tell me something, General. Do you remember a

farm in Croatia, summer of 1994? You burned it to the ground. Killed a family. Mother, father, brother, daughter. Ring any bells?"

"There were many of those, young lady."

"It was just another day to you, wasn't it?"

"Your family? You're doing this to me for revenge?"

She laughed, a low, throaty laugh without humor. "You act like *you're* the victim, Dragoslav. Ridiculous."

"It's General *Nikolic* to you."

"Whatever, Draggy, baby."

She watched his face twitch. His right hand twitched, too. He wanted to hit her. But his tactical mind took over at the last second and prevented the movement. He knew she was trying to break through his barriers; he wasn't going to let her. If he determined a victory through her slight grin, he didn't show it, either.

"I don't remember many slipping through my fingers, young lady. Either fate smiled upon you, or you were better and faster than the rest of your family. Hmmm? And now what? You've come for revenge. To kill me? Hardly. You're at my mercy, young lady."

"And you're at mine, General."

"I am?"

"All I have to do is sit here and shiver until my people show up. You think I'm helpless? You have no idea."

"Where are your friends?"

She shook her head. "You're getting scared, aren't you? You have this fortress, your guards, but you're jumping at shadows. You don't even know who's coming for you. You have no idea how big the force I've spent—"

She didn't get to finish. This time, Nikolic's tactical sense had no power over raw fury.

He smacked her across the face with one hand and punched her in the gut with the other. Elena wretched onto her lap and her face flared with pain. After a coughing fit, she forced herself to raise her head and laugh.

It hurt to laugh, but it was better than screaming.

A distant thud shook the villa. The vibrations rattled Elena's chair. The general forgot his anger. His expression changed to surprise. Another thud followed. The bulb above flickered, dust sifting from the ceiling. Nikolic turned as one of his men hurried down the steps and burst into the room.

"We're under attack! Helicopters—multiple! They're hitting the perimeter!"

Nikolic's eyes widened, then arrowed as he turned back to Elena.

She said, "I didn't need no tracking device, General. Get my clothes, huh?"

The Wolf instead pivoted and the guard ran ahead of him.

Pain radiated from her stomach and face, but the distant booms grew louder now. Rockets, gunfire, the unmistakable roar of helicopter rotors. Raven and Hasanaj. They'd found her, somehow. The swinging bulb above swung wildly now, and shadows danced around the walls.

Elena's lips curled. Nikolic assumed she was helpless, but he'd underestimated her—and her friends. Raven and Hasanaj were carving a path to her, and when they arrived, she'd turn the basement into The Wolf's tomb. She only had to hold on a little longer.

37

Four large combat choppers roared across the treetops, their rotors thumping a war drum through the night. Each carried a squad of Hasanaj's volunteer commandos. Raven crouched near the open side door of the lead chopper. Wind whipped at his face and tactical vest. He'd finally traded his Uzi for an HK416, the carbine issued to all of the fighters in the helicopters. He wore the weapon strapped across his chest. Hasanaj kneeled beside him with NVGs pushed up on his forehead. The other three choppers flanked them, the silhouettes of each flying machine bristling with rocket pods and machine guns. They were bringing war to The Wolf's doorstep.

"Two minutes to target."

The pilot's voice crackled over Raven's headset. He glanced at Hasanaj, who gave a curt nod. They had a simple plan. Soften the villa's defenses with an airborne assault, then land and storm the compound to extract Elena and finish off the cartel boss for good. Raven had no plans to take Nikolic alive. There'd be no trial in The Hague. The Wolf was walking dead, but didn't know it yet.

Nikolic's security was no joke, according to Ana Gray's intelligence. Sentries, full-auto cannons on the roof, rumored anti-aircraft missiles. Raven's jaw tightened. They'd hit hard, hit fast, and accomplish the mission. The odds were against them, though. But he'd never let such odds deter him before. There was always a way, especially if you fired first, and crippled your opponent before he had a chance to respond.

The choppers crested the final ridge, and the villa came into view, a glittering jewel in the blanket of green surrounding it. In the dark of the night, the green trees had no definition; the villa appeared to be floating in space.

"Engage!" Hasanaj barked the order into his com unit. The lead chopper's nose dipped, and a pair of high-explosive air-to-ground missiles streaked from left- and right-mounted rocket pods. The missiles screamed toward the villa's outer wall. Explosions bloomed, orange and white, shattering concrete and hurling debris skyward. Screams echoed faintly as cartel troopers scrambled for cover. The other three choppers followed the lead's example, firing their own rockets which slammed into guard towers and a parked Jeep at the side, which erupted in a fireball and lit the property for a brief instant.

"Gunners, now!" Hasanaj shouted. The door gunners opened fire, machine guns chattering as they raked the villa's grounds. Tracers arced like deadly fireflies, cutting down cartel troopers who took a stand in the open and returned fire with their AK-74s. A rooftop turret swiveled toward the lead chopper, its autocannon spitting rounds, but the second chopper's gunner zeroed it, shredding the emplacement with a hail of hot tracers resembling sci-fi laser bolts against the dark sky. Raven gripped the doorframe handles, the chopper banking hard as it completed the first pass. Below, the villa's lawns were scarred, flames licking at shattered outbuildings, but the main structure stood defiant, its walls barely scratched. Raven wondered if Nikolic had evacuated or not.

"Second pass!" Hasanaj ordered. His voice remained steady despite the chaos. The helicopters swung around, skimming low over the treetops once more. Raven spotted movement—guards regrouping near the villa's east wing and carrying a shoulder-fired missile launcher. "Stinger, three o'clock low!" he yelled. The chopper's gunner pivoted, unleashing a burst. Flame flashed from the muzzle, and the gunner was on target. The burst turned the launcher crew into red mist.

The third chopper let loose another rocket salvo, this one targeting the villa's generator housing. The blast sent a shockwave through the property; the lights everywhere, house and grounds, flickered and died, plunging the compound into darkness save for the fires.

Hasanaj leaned closer to Raven. "Thermal scans show hostiles still in the main building. Heat signature in the basement is likely Elena. But Raven?"

"What?" Raven snapped.

"She's not moving."

Raven nodded. He said nothing. Not moving but registering a heat signature didn't mean dead. But if The Wolf had harmed her in such a way as to incapacitate her permanently, he'd tear the Serbian bastard apart one piece at a time.

The choppers climbed for altitude, evading small-arms fire pinging off their hulls. A surface-to-air missile streaked from the villa's west side, the contrail a glowing snake. Raven shouted a warning, but the flight crew was already reacting. The pilot juked left, deploying flares from the rear of the chopper. The flares burst like miniature suns, and the missile veered off, exploding into the forest.

"We gotta land," the pilot said over the coms, "before they shoot another!"

"Copy," Raven said.

"Prep for drop!" Hasanaj called out. The commandos—eight per chopper, their faces blackened, eyes granite hard—checked weapons and their rappelling gear. Hasanaj pulled down his NVGs.

"Primary target is Elena," Raven said.

If she's still alive...

But Raven wasn't going to consider the possibility until he saw her with his own eyes.

The choppers descended. When the lead helicopter reached twenty feet above ground, Raven clipped his fast-rope to the hook above the door and kicked out into the night. He slid down, boots hitting grass littered with debris, and jammed the HK416 to his shoulder to sweep for targets. He spotted a lone trooper sprinting for cover, yelling to concealed comrades. Raven's single shot dropped the man.

Hasanaj landed beside him, and the choppers then disgorged the rest of the commandos. They rode down their zip lines like so many spiders, fanning out in practiced formation. The choppers kept enemy heads down with criss-crossing streams of tracer fire from the door gunners of each.

The second chopper took ground fire, its door gunner returning the favor with a withering burst, silencing the threat. The hail of bullets tore into the low wall the cartel gunners hid behind, chunks of plaster mingling with the bloody bodies.

"Perimeter teams, secure the east and west," Hasanaj ordered. "Raven! With me. Main entrance!"

Explosions still echoed from the villa's edges, where the choppers' final rockets salvos had cratered the driveways, but the commandos moved with lethal focus, their weapons crackling as they cleared stragglers.

Raven and Hasanaj sprinted to the villa's rear entrance,

shattered glass crunching under their boots as they reached the patio, chunks of debris creating obstacles to avoid. Both kept their HK416s at the ready. A cartel trooper burst from the clutter and shadows to the right of the patio doors. The guard never got a chance to fire his weapon. Raven tagged him chest-high with a 3-round burst of 5.56mm tumblers. The trooper fell back, sending a wild burst from his SMG into the sky.

Hasanaj lobbed a grenade through the half-blown-off patio doors. The blast shook one of the doors off the hinges and it landed with a sharp crash on the concrete patio. The smuggler moved up against the wall beside the door. Raven entered first and cut right; Hasanaj followed, cutting left. The room was a mess of rubble and bleeding bodies and groans of the wounded. Chandeliers hung dark. But they heard movement. Shuffling footsteps. Despite the scattered shooting still taking place outside, Raven's senses picked up the close-quarter threats. The room led to a narrow hallway opening on a wider area of the house, and Raven and Hasanaj paused. They took cover behind crumbled chunks. They were walking into pitch black. Hasanaj used his NVGs to scan ahead but then lifted the goggles from his eyes and shook his head at Raven.

All right, then, Raven decided, *grenades it is.*

He plucked a high-explosive frag grenade from his combat vest. Hasanaj did likewise. They tossed at the same time.

38

THE GRENADE BLASTS SHOOK THE WALLS, DUST DRIFTED down, and chandeliers fell with a crash. "Go!" Raven said. He and Hasanaj moved into the dark, the only illumination coming from the lights mounted on the ends of the carbines.

Raven's HK416 carbine swept the shadows as he scanned for threats. Hasanaj moved beside him, weapon at the ready, his night-vision goggles casting a faint green glow.

"Basement's our target," Hasanaj whispered.

"You don't need to remind me," Raven said.

He followed the beam of light from his weapon. The villa's opulence—gilded frames, velvet drapes—felt like a grotesque mask over the bloodshed it housed.

A burst of gunfire erupted from the left corridor, and two cartel troopers appeared, their AKs blazing. Raven dove behind a marble pillar, bullets chipping stone above his head. Hasanaj dropped to a knee, firing two precise shots, catching the troopers in the chest and throat. They crumpled, blood pooling beneath a shattered vase.

"Move!" Raven barked.

They advanced, stepping over bodies, the air heavy with the coppery scent of death.

The corridor opened into a grand atrium, its glass dome cracked from a stray rocket. Moonlight filtered through, illuminating Anton Vercuni and his wife, Melika, positioned behind an overturned oak table. Anton clutched a Beretta 92, his custom Damascus steel knife glinting at his hip. Melika wielded a compact MP5, her eyes cold and calculating. Four cartel enforcers flanked them, one of them the big man Raven recognized, their weapons trained on the corridor's mouth. Raven and Hasanaj dropped low, using a bullet-riddled sofa as cover.

Melika fired a burst from her MP5, the rounds shredding the sofa's upholstery. Raven rolled left, returning fire with his HK416, catching one enforcer in the shoulder. The man screamed, dropping his weapon, but the others unleashed a barrage, forcing Raven and Hasanaj to scatter. Hasanaj crawled forward, using a fallen statue for cover, and lobbed a flashbang. The detonation filled the atrium with blinding light and a deafening crack, disorienting the cartel fighters.

Hasanaj seized the moment, rising and firing. His HK416 barked, dropping Dede Bizi and the trooper next to him with headshots. The big man's *thud* on the ground seemed louder than any earlier explosion. Melika pivoted, her MP5 tracking the smuggler, but Hasanaj was faster. He snapped off a single round, the bullet punching through her throat. She staggered, blood spraying from either end of her throat, and collapsed, her weapon clattering to the floor. Anton roared, his Beretta blazing as he emptied the magazine at the smuggler. Bullets tore through the sofa, one grazing Hasanaj's arm, a hot sting he ignored. The Beretta's slide locked back, empty, and Anton cursed, tossing it aside. He drew his custom knife, its serrated edge catching the moonlight, and charged.

Raven met him head-on and shouted for the smuggler to find Elena. Anton was fast, his knife slashing toward Raven's ribs, but Raven sidestepped, deflecting the knife with the stock of the HK416. The cartel operative snarled, driving a knee into Raven's gut. Pain flared, but Raven held firm, slamming his elbow into Anton's jaw. The knife clattered to the floor, and Anton slammed into Raven's midsection. Raven lost his grip on the HK and it dangled alongside him. They shuffled back. Raven didn't want to end up on the floor. The two men grappled, fists and knees flying in a brutal dance. Anton's strength was surprising, fueled by rage, but Raven was a machine of controlled violence. He hooked Anton's leg, sending him crashing to the floor, and straddled him. A punch to the face kept Anton dizzy while Raven snatched his own Ka-Bar knife from the sheath on his leg and drove it into Anton's heart. Vercuni gasped, eyes wide, then went still.

The atrium fell silent. Even the fighting outside sounded like it had subsided. Raven rose, wiped the knife on Anton Vercuni's suit, and put the Ka-Bar away. Retrieving his HK416, he found Hasanaj nearby, having stayed behind to cover the American instead of leaving him alone.

"Basement," Raven said. "Let's move."

Hasanaj led the way this time. They navigated a maze of corridors, the villa's grandeur giving way to utilitarian concrete as they descended a stairwell. A lone guard appeared at the bottom of the stairs, raising his weapon, but Hasanaj's quick shot dropped him before he could fire. The basement door loomed, heavy steel, partially ajar. Raven signaled for quiet, his pulse steady but urgent. Elena was close.

They kicked open the door. It slammed against the opposite wall. The pair entered, weapons raised and froze. General Dragoslav Nikolic—The Wolf—stood in the center of the basement, a CZ-75 pistol pressed against Elena's temple. She was naked, freed from the chair, her wrists red from restraints. Nikolic held her in front of him as a shield, one arm locked around her throat, her body tense but defiant. The single bulb overhead swung, casting jagged shadows across the concrete.

"Let her go, Nikolic," Raven said, his HK416 steady, laser dot dancing on the general's shoulder—the only clear shot. "It's over. Your villa's burning and your men are dead."

Nikolic's hair gleamed under the bulb, his eyes like a predator's, unyielding. "The American," he growled, tightening his grip on Elena. "You've got guts, coming here. You'll watch her die. I'll end her like I ended her family."

Elena's eyes met Raven's, a flicker of trust amid her fear. She spoke. Her voice was hoarse but defiant. "He's alone, Raven. No one's coming to help him."

Nikolic pressed the pistol harder against her temple, his lips curling. "Shut up, little girl."

Raven's mind raced for a solution. Any shot risked Elena but waiting gave Nikolic control. The standoff stretched, seconds bleeding into eternity, the basement's chill seeping into their bones.

Elena acted first. With a sudden twist, she drove her elbow into Nikolic's ribs, loosening his grip. She ducked, exposing his chest, and Raven didn't hesitate. His HK416 barked, a single round punching through Nikolic's forehead. The general's head snapped back, blood spraying, and he collapsed, the CZ-75 clattering to the floor. The basement fell silent, the bulb still swinging, casting wild shadows over the carnage.

Raven rushed to Elena, slinging his rifle and pulling a tactical jacket from his pack to cover her. "You okay?"

She nodded, shivering but resolute. "Took you long enough," she said, a weak smile breaking through her exhaustion. Hasanaj joined them, handing her a spare pistol from his belt. "We need to get out of here," he said, checking his watch.

Raven supported Elena as they climbed the stairs. The villa was a warzone, flames licking the upper floors, smoke choking the corridors. They emerged into the night, the helicopters waiting on the scarred lawn, rotors spinning. Raven helped Elena aboard, Hasanaj covering their rear as the squads piled in. The choppers lifted off, the villa shrinking below, a pyre against the Serbian mountains. Elena gripped Raven's hand; her eyes were fixed on the horizon.

The Wolf was dead, but the war wasn't over. The war never ended. It was only the conclusion of the current fight. But for now, they could rest.

39

ELENA'S EYES OPENED. DIM LIGHT FILTERED THROUGH THE
curtains casting soft shadows across the unfamiliar room.
For a fleeting moment, she thought it was a dream. A nightmare spun from the darkest corners of her mind. The
gunfire, the blood, Nikolic's sneer as he loomed over her, the
searing pain of his fist against her body. Her heart lurched,
and she squeezed her eyes shut, willing the images to
dissolve into the ether of sleep. But the dull ache throbbing
in her side, the tight pull of bandages wrapped around her
arm, and the sharp sting of a cut on her cheek told a different
story. This was no dream. It was real, and she survived.

She lay still, her breath shallow, as if moving too quickly
might unravel the fragile thread holding her together. The
bed was soft, the sheets clean and crisp, a stark contrast to
the gritty chaos of the cartel's compound. Her fingers
brushed the edge of a bandage on her ribs, the adhesive
tugging at her skin. Raven had gotten her out. Raven, with
his steely eyes and unrelenting precision, had stormed
through the hail of bullets to pull her from the jaws of death.
She owed him her life. Him and Hasanaj. She couldn't forget

Kemal. But the weight of that debt sat heavy in her chest, mingling with the guilt gnawing at her from inside.

What had she been thinking, going after Nikolic alone? The plan had been reckless, a suicide mission born of rage and desperation. Emotion had overruled good sense, a tidal wave of vengeance for the lives Nikolic had destroyed—her mother, her father, her siblings—and every soul crushed under his empire of drugs. She'd wanted to be the one to end him, to feel the satisfaction of watching the light fade from his eyes. Instead, she'd nearly gotten herself killed, forcing Raven to clean up her mess.

Her lips pressed into a thin line as she stared at the ceiling, the plaster cracked in a way that reminded her of her own fractured resolve. Raven probably wouldn't want to see her again. Not after she'd gone rogue. She could picture his face, the hard set of his jaw, the way his silence spoke louder than any reprimand. He was a professional, a man who thrived on control, and she'd been a wildfire, burning through carefully discussed plans. *It doesn't matter*, she told herself, though the thought stung more than she cared to admit. The mission was over. Nikolic was dead, his empire teetering on the edge of collapse. But still a threat.

Elena shifted slightly, wincing as a sharp pain lanced through her. She thought of Ana Gray, the woman who'd pulled her into this shadow world of spies and secrets. Ana's private network was a lifeline, a chance to fight the kind of evil governments ignored or enabled. Nikolic's death would leave a power vacuum, a gaping wound in the cartel's structure others would scramble to fill; they couldn't let it happen. Ana would need her—bandaged, battered, but unbroken—to help dismantle what remained of Nikolic's network. There were lieutenants still out there, ambitious and ruthless, ready to carve up the empire for themselves. Elena's work wasn't done. It might never be done.

She considered getting up, swinging her legs over the side of the bed, and forcing herself to move. But her body protested, every muscle heavy with exhaustion, every bone aching with the memory of the fight. For once, she listened to it. She deserved this moment, this small rebellion against the relentless pace of her life. She reached for the blanket, pulling it up to her chin, then over her head, cocooning herself in its warmth. The world could wait a little longer.

In the quiet darkness beneath the covers, she let her mind settle. The crawling sensation—the "bugs"—were gone. No phantom skittering across her skin, no imagined whispers in her ears. Their absence was a victory, hard-won and fragile, but hers. She clung to it, letting it anchor her as her breathing slowed. *Rest*, she thought. *Just for now*. The fight would be there when she woke, but this moment was hers to claim.

"HOW IS SHE?"

Raven stood outside the safehouse once again, phone to his ear, listening to Ana Gray's voice. His expression had softened since their return to the safehouse. They were exhausted, drained, in need of sleep, and while Raven had stolen a few hours to let his body recharge, his mind wouldn't rest until he settled the last stray details.

"She'll be okay," he told her. His explanation of the fight took a few minutes, and he left out how she slipped out of the house to finish the fight herself. He understood why she did it and regretted he hadn't been there to convince her not to. It was something Ana didn't need to know. He'd hold it from her the way she held things from him.

"What now?" Ana asked.

Raven chuckled. "I told you I was tired."

"The cartel isn't finished."

"You'll think of something. I'm out of it. For now. If it gets hot again, you know how to reach me. In the meantime, you have other assets. Use them."

"Okay."

"Ana?"

"Yes?"

"Hasanaj is a good man."

"I understand."

"Talk to you soon."

Raven ended the call and turned to start for the house but stopped. Kemal Hasanaj stood on the porch, holding a cup of coffee, watching him.

"I appreciate the compliment," he said.

"It's well deserved," Raven said. He joined the smuggler. "We couldn't have done this without you."

"She thinks I want the spoils, doesn't she?"

"She did."

Hasanaj laughed. "I don't need it. My organization is fine as it is. I have my tailoring business. I have all I need, Raven. And I like being one of Ana's secret weapons."

"You should tell her."

"Maybe I will. Maybe—"

"You won't?"

"I also like the idea of nobody being quite convinced of what side I'm on."

"It's overrated," Raven said. "Trust me."

Hasanaj sipped his coffee. "When do you want to get her out of bed?"

Raven shook his head. "Let her sleep. We have one more stop to make before I leave, but it can wait a bit."

"I have more coffee inside."

"Any tea?"

"There's tea, too."

"I'll make some tea, and we can talk shop all we want."

"Sounds fine."

Hasanaj held the door for Raven, and they went inside.

THE HOSPITAL ROOM was a sterile cage where Lieutenant Vojin Stojanovic lay tethered to an IV drip and the weight of his choices. The bandages across his chest and thigh were tight, a constant reminder of the bullets fired into his body during his one-man raid on Anton Vercuni's house. The pain was dull now, blunted by medication, but it flared with every breath, as if his body refused to let him forget.

He stared at the ceiling, counting the tiles for the hundredth time, when the door creaked open. Captain Rostoder stepped inside, his uniform crisp, his face etched with a mix of concern and disapproval.

"Vojin," Rostoder said, his voice low but firm, like a father addressing a wayward son. "You look like hell."

Stojanovic managed a weak chuckle. "Feel like it, too, Captain." He gestured to the chair by the bed. "Sit. Unless you're here to arrest me."

Rostoder's lips twitched, but he didn't smile. He sat, folding his hands in his lap, his eyes scanning Stojanovic like a detective sizing up a suspect. "Why'd you do it, Vojin? Storming Vercuni's place alone, no backup, no plan. What were you hoping to accomplish?"

Stojanovic's jaw tightened. He'd rehearsed this moment in his head, but the truth was a tangle of half-truths and lies. "I got a tip," he said, his voice steady despite the ache in his chest. "Vercuni was tied to the Vukovic murder. I wanted to bring him in myself. Make it clean."

"Clean?" Rostoder's brow arched. "You nearly died. For

what? A personal vendetta? You're a lieutenant, not a vigilante."

Stojanovic looked away, his gaze settling on the window where the city's lights flickered in the dusk.

"Vercuni's still out there," Stojanovic muttered, more to himself than Rostoder. "Running free."

Rostoder leaned forward, his voice dropping. "No, he's not. Vercuni, Melika, the man we've identified as the mysterious boss—they're all dead. So are dozens of their soldiers. Happened in Serbia. Some kind of bloodbath. We're still piecing it together, but there's no one left to talk. The Balkan Cartel's done, Vojin. Smashed."

Stojanovic's breath caught, his mind racing. Dead. All of them. *The two men at the house...*

The American in particular.

The news should have been a relief. He should have felt a weight rising off his shoulders. No one was left to expose him, to whisper that Lieutenant Vojin Stojanovic had been a cartel informant. He was free. Yet the guilt remained like a stone lodged in his gut. He'd betrayed his badge, his oath, even if it was to keep his wife alive. The blood on his hands wasn't just from the raid.

"You don't look happy," Rostoder said, his eyes narrowing. "Thought you'd be relieved."

Stojanovic forced a thin smile. "Just tired, Captain. It's been a long fight."

Rostoder studied him for a long moment, then stood, adjusting his cap. "Get well, Vojin. We need you back on the force. Your full attention this time." The words hung in the air, heavy with unspoken meaning. Did Rostoder know? Had he suspected all along Stojanovic was playing both sides? The captain's face gave nothing away, but the weight of his gaze felt like a warning.

"I'll be there," Stojanovic said, his voice firm despite the uncertainty gnawing at him. "Ready to start fresh."

Rostoder nodded and left. The door clicked shut, and Stojanovic exhaled, sinking into the pillows. The cartel was gone, his secrets buried with it. This was his second chance, a clean slate he didn't deserve but would seize with both hands. He closed his eyes, the city's hum a faint lullaby, and vowed to make things right.

THE CEMETERY in Podgorica stretched out in quiet rows, a patchwork of stone and memory beneath a slate-gray sky. Raven stood before Irina Vukovic's grave, his hands clasped, his face carved from granite. The gravestone was simple, unadorned save for her name and dates; the brevity of her life etched in stark letters. Fresh flowers, roses and lilies, lay scattered at its base, their petals vibrant against the muted earth. The grave was still fresh. Her family, wherever they were, still in the early stages of grief. Elena stood to his left, her bandaged arm held close, her eyes tracing the stone with a mix of sorrow and resolve. Hasanaj, his weathered face softened by his own reflection, flanked Raven's right. His silence was heavier than words.

"She was very brave," Elena said, her voice low, cutting through the stillness. "The kind of brave the world needs more of. Not many would've done what she did."

Hasanaj nodded, his gaze fixed on the flowers. "She deserved better."

Raven's jaw tightened, his eyes never leaving the stone. Irina's face flickered in his mind. Her fierce determination, her quiet strength. He'd fought to keep her from the line of fire, but the cartel's reach had been too long—or was he making excuses?

Maybe you simply screwed up, dude. She was another to join the ghosts of battles past. She's whispered to him in the quiet moments, same as the others, those he couldn't save, urging him on, demanding he keep fighting for those who couldn't fight for themselves. Somebody who could win when they couldn't.

It was a war without end. The end would only come when Raven stopped a bullet. No sooner, no later.

Hasanaj placed a hand on Raven's shoulder. Raven turned to him. The smuggler only nodded. Raven still didn't speak. There was nothing he wanted to say. He only wanted to get back in the fight. Back to the war.

A gentle breeze stirred, rustling the leaves of the nearby oaks, carrying the faint scent of the flowers. Birds chirped from the branches, their song a soft counterpoint to the solemnity below. The air felt lighter, as if the earth itself offered a moment of peace. But only a moment. Peace never lasted for long.

A LOOK AT:

OCTOBER BLOOD (JACK SLAYTON 1)

This Ex-Navy SEAL still serves his Country.

Three years ago, CIA specialist and former Navy SEAL Jack Slayton lost everything when Reema Ashraf—the woman he loved and the partner he trusted with his life—vanished during a covert mission gone catastrophically wrong. The world believes she died. Jack knows the truth only because he sees her in every nightmare… and because he never stopped searching.

Then Reema returns. Her appearance is as shocking as the message she brings: a warning wrapped in riddles, pointing to a rogue intelligence syndicate operating in the shadows of Europe, and embedded deep within the very agencies sworn to protect American lives. Someone inside their circle orchestrated her disappearance. Someone wants them both dead.

Catapulted into a relentless chase through the criminal underworld, Jack and Reema must navigate double-crosses, buried loyalties, and a global conspiracy whose reach is far greater than either imagined. As Jack races to stop a terror plot engineered by those who should be allies, he must also confront a devastating truth: wanting someone back doesn't mean you're ready for what comes with them.

The countdown has started. The betrayals are personal. And for Jack Slayton, winning isn't enough.

He must reign supreme.

AVAILABLE FEBRUARY 2026

ABOUT THE AUTHOR

A twenty-five year veteran of radio and television broadcasting, Brian Drake has spent his career in San Francisco where he's filled writing, producing, and reporting duties with stations such as KPIX-TV, KCBS, KQED, among many others. Currently carrying out sports and traffic reporting duties for Bloomberg 960, Brian Drake spends time between reports and carefully guarded morning and evening hours cranking out action/adventure tales.

A love of reading when he was younger inspired him to create his own stories, and he sold his first short story, "The Desperate Minutes," to an obscure webzine when he was 25 (more years ago than he cares to remember, so don't ask).

Brian Drake lives in California with his wife and two cats, and when he's not writing he is usually blasting along the back roads in his Corvette with his wife telling him not to drive so fast, but the engine is so loud he usually can't hear her.

briandrakebooks.com